Hillbilly *Hell*thcare

Written by Jodi Renfroe

Published by Jodi Renfroe Books 2022©

Printed in the United States of America

ISBN-9798795881591

Library of Congress Control Number-TBD

Author Website-www.hillbillyhellthcare.com

Editing and formatting in collaboration with Jeffrey A. Mangus-CEO Ghostwriting USA

http://www.ghostwritingusa.com
http://www.Jeffreymangus.com

Table of Contents

Contents

Prologue
Eastern Kentucky
1978

We were early as usual. There were misshapen ladies in flowered dresses, pantyhose, and orthopedic shoes already scattered along the concrete steps when we arrived. A one-room church sat atop a raised basement Sunday school. The building was white clapboard with a small steeple-enclosed bell atop. My mom finished her cigarette in the front seat of our Pontiac, then hustled me in, banjo in tow.

This was the final stop on our whirlwind tour of church revivals. There had been tents and schoolhouses, picnic shelters, and community centers, but all the preachers said that the people were the church, not the buildings. This preacher was a thin, middle-aged man with a scary glass eye that sat in place like a crystal ball, but he seemed nice and told me how happy he was that I was visiting.

We only went to Bible-believing churches. Baptist, Holiness, maybe Methodist if we knew them and knew they weren't hypocrites or heathens in disguise. God had given me the gift of music, so my mom was careful how it was used. I still got nervous before I played, resulting in the urge to pee, and that day was no different. Up in the pews, I was squirming around, and my mom could tell. I'd been trying to hold it because I'd seen the outhouse, and I was afraid of opossums, but a kind woman told us they'd just gotten indoor plumbing.

I descended the stairs to the Sunday school bathroom with minutes to spare before the service. The area was still unfinished, with a single exposed lightbulb hanging down at the base of the stairwell. Darkness enveloped the remaining hallway beyond. There was a square of light shining through a clouded basement bathroom window. I stepped onto the concrete floor and heard the rattling, but the strike was over before I could react.

Awakening after what felt like hours or days but may have only been seconds or minutes, I held the snake, still alive and writhing, in my left hand. My right hand lay paralyzed and wounded. In the darkness, I could see the outlines of the cages enclosing the other vipers, could hear the anointing with oils upstairs, the speaking in tongues. I heard my mother's voice, frantic and rising. I slipped back into blackness and saw sadness and despair, a bad dream.

Mark 16:17, 18 And these signs will follow those who believe: In My name, they will cast out demons; they will speak with new tongues; they will take up serpents...

Chapter 1: 2020

I was out of work again. I had a home improvement loan and a car payment to worry about (newly purchased, of course.) I'd been a dietitian with the same hospital for 15 years, was in my late forties, and had to start all over. People told me to go into healthcare because it was safe and I'd always have a job, but this hospital was shutting down, and they had given us a prognosis of less than a year before they pulled the plug.

I headed over to my mom's house to pick up my daughter. Mom was on the porch of her double-wide, an Elmo-print "dew rag" covering the majority of her hair. The look was a holdover from her days working down at the convenience store deli, where she'd made biscuits and gravy for the morning-shift work crews. There wasn't a construction worker, lineman, bus driver, or much of anyone in the county with a job who hadn't savored her cooking. She'd recently retired, to the dismay of many a customer.

"I saw on the news. What you gonna do?" she asked between drags.

"I've got something lined up. Just as good or better," I said, really meaning it at that point.

"Well, you wouldn't have to work at all if that deadbeat ex-husband of yours didn't break the law," she countered.

"I know, Mom, I know."

"I just don't see why you couldn't have married Jesse," she dreamt aloud, talking about Jesse Palmer from her favorite Food Network show, *Holiday Baking Championship*. Mom had been watching a lot of TV since she retired.

"Which of my reasons you want today?" I asked. The reasons were always the same. He was at the University of Florida almost a decade after me. I was way older than him, I was only there one semester, and I'd never even met him. Instead of getting into it all, I just moved on.

"Thanks for watching Sid," I said. "Let's not tell her about the hospital 'cause she'll worry."

"Okay, but don't call her that, I tell ya."

Mom was against the name Sidney, said it could be a boy's name, and people might make it short and call my daughter "Sid," which, she said, is definitely a boy's name.

"Okay, Mom!" I agreed, just to avoid a fight.

The car packed up, we headed out to the farm, Sid telling me about her day and me keeping my day all to myself.

That night I lay awake in bed, thinking back to 2005 when I returned to Appalachia, another point where I'd had to start my life over once again. I'd been married and living out in California, but I had to move fast to get away, so I packed up a U-Haul with essentials and left in the night. Three days later, exhausted and underwhelmed, I pulled in at the two-story house my great aunt and uncle once inhabited.

Nothing had been done to the house since they died in the eighties. It was, essentially, a money pit. One contractor told me it would cost twenty-five cents to fix the house: "Just buy a box of matches and burn it down." That contractor wasn't wrong, but I was pulled in by a need to reconnect to my past. Moving back to the family farm and renovating the homeplace was romantic and noble, and I needed a project to busy my mind. So, I started fixing up the old farmhouse and found two part-time jobs within weeks of my re-entry into Appalachian society. As I prepared to start another new chapter in my life, I lay awake in a cozy room in that very farmhouse. Anything was possible.

My ex-husband had been a college women's soccer coach turned college admissions expert-cum-millionaire and expert of college women, if you know what I mean. But that college admissions scandal thing? He was busted on that way before it became a documentary. Listen, I wasn't sayin' I was perfect, but the things I had done didn't typically hurt other people. *ALL* have sinned and come short of the glory of God (Romans 3:23). I had my secrets.

My mom 100% despised my ex, of course. It was less for what he did (violating multiple biblical commandments like lying, stealing, and adultery), but more for the fact that she got taken in by him, too. She prided herself on being able to read people. She was a skeptic by nature, and he won her over. Con artist. Also, my mom didn't understand why I wanted to marry him, so scrawny and average, when "you could have anybody!" Mom always thought I was the smartest and the prettiest. And she (ironically) didn't like that he smoked.

About those jobs: One was through a medical consulting agency, completing nutrition audits on nursing home charts in a blocky windowless office. The other was to cover shifts for vacationing dietitians at Our Lady of the River, a Catholic hospital about forty minutes from my secluded farm. Our Lady was excellent. The nursing home not so much. Because I was new with the consulting company, I was doomed to be sent to the facility nobody wanted.

My first day on the consulting job was capped off with a sobbing call to the agency with a plea for relocation (it didn't happen). The nursing staff at the home tried to reassure me that it isn't an everyday occurrence a geriatric-psychiatric patient runs through the plate glass naked. Just on rare occasions, like my first day. And no amount of bleach could erase the pungent smell of urine that assaulted you upon entrance. Freedom Nursing Home, in fact, had been investigated by the state regulatory agencies just before my introduction as a dietitian. This was, unfortunately, due to a patient choking on a cheese sandwich, leading to an untimely death. The patient was supposed to be on a puree diet!

About two months into my nursing home career, I showed up to Freedom on a bright, sunny Monday morning, threw open the double doors of that smelly lobby, and found stacks of files and cardboard boxes being hauled out by dark-suited men. There was no acknowledgment of my presence until one familiar face emerged, a nurse's aide.

"The state shut us down, moved all the patients by bus to Cleveland last night," said the nurse's aide as she passed me on her way out. After that, it was all about Our Lady.

Chapter 2: Hospitals

Our Lady, being a Catholic Hospital in Appalachia (Eastern Kentucky, to be exact), was really an anomaly considering 99% of area residents were non-Catholic Christian-professing people. Christian-professing and actual Christian were two different things. Christian-professing and anti-Catholic were in some cases the same thing. For example, right before Easter every year, the effigies of Jesus would disappear from the elevators, leaving empty crosses behind. The "good ole boys" in the break room found this hilarious, but many devout Christians found it either wrong (stealing is no better than idolatry) or justified.

My family didn't want me working there at first.

"It's Catholic!" protested Aunt Henny.

"They's a statue of Mary out front of there!" gasped my cousin, Jasper.

There was also a third cousin who grabbed me in the canned food aisle of the Pic-N-Save one evening to express her displeasure.

"They killed my aunt!" she said. But I knew Mamie was 97 years old when she passed, so I didn't lend much credence to the claim.

But they also didn't want me to be one of those people who "took welfare," so we had agreed that God worked in mysterious ways, and maybe I was being put there for a reason. The truth was, I was already a black sheep and unacceptable in the church's eyes because I was DIVORCED. I promised that if they started worshiping Mary there, I would immediately quit my job.

There weren't any nuns at the hospital anymore, like in the fifties, before I was even born, back when the hospital services included the delivery of babies. By the time I came fully on the scene, Our Lady was more of a grown-ups-only hospital, mostly serving a mission to help the poor and needy.

Helping the poor and needy was something Megadocs, the gleaming modern hospital downtown, was not apt to do. Megadocs was a gigantic hospital and medical center with every possible outpatient service, medical test, and the latest equipment needed to perform it all. Megadocs was a money-making machine, while modest Our Lady skirted by on community donations and fundraising. There were always employee campaigns yearly, where janitors, food handlers, respiratory therapists, and doctors would all come together to buy equipment for the operating room or tiles for the lobby. Our Lady was like an underdog community college team going up against a giant state university, and every player was giving 100% just to keep us in the game. When Our Lady tried to expand services to include heart procedures, Megadocs took it straight to court, burying the plan in attorney's fees.

My defining moment with Our Lady came in March 2007, when I was hired from part-time to full-time as a dietitian and Clinical Nutrition Manager. There was cake and punch and a reception in the boardroom. Because it was such a great place to work, turnover was practically nil at Our Lady. I had that opportunity only because my contemporary was stepping into an upper management position left vacant due to retirement. Employees were valued. We were cherished. I would be sent to headquarters in Baltimore, Maryland, for Catholic leadership training. Over those next few years, I was molded into the image of a mission-driven, caring servant leader, learning a lot about the geography of West Virginia in the process.

My traveling companions on the Baltimore trips were other middle managers, most of whom were also locally born. Every seven-hour drive to Baltimore was filled with lively conversation about work and family and segmented with infrequently spaced pee breaks at rural West Virginia exits like Big Otter. When a rest area was advertised, the opportunity was seized, lest desperation set in, even to the point of pulling over on the side of the road to pee, blocked by open car doors and held-up blankets compliments of the other passengers.

Eating could also be a problem if mealtimes weren't planned out correctly. One trip back, we misjudged our location, exiting deep into the coalfields searching for fast food. It was there, about three miles in and directly beside a bustling strip club with a flashing marquee advertising what I won't repeat, that we found our restaurant chain. Everybody had to pee so badly that we flew inside and up the restroom hallway to find two restaurant employees in a full make-out session, blocking the door. We all just pushed them aside and went into the filthy lavatory. We were on a mission. No food was purchased there. After bagged chips and canned pop were procured from a filthy convenience store, we filled up with gas and were back on the road.

We bonded over our opinions on local news stories. "You think that woman's just after money?" This question was asked as we listened to the local radio station recount a happening at CapMed, a hospital an hour away from our own.

"I don't know. She did get a lawyer," I had replied.

The young woman claimed she was in the waiting area when another patient groped her. She had complained to hospital administrators and security, but they did nothing to help her, so she called the police. Then she contacted an attorney.

"All the training we have to go through at hospitals, how could that *really* happen?" a man in our group had asked.

13

Every year a fun ice cream social was held in the picnic area between the hospital and the parking garage, and we also had a cookout at least once a year. There were Christmas bonuses of crisp one-hundred-dollar bills and sometimes even a ham. Movie gift cards were showered upon worthy recipients as a form of praise or on everybody for special occasions. People were friendly to each other! Traditions were big at Our Lady, and I'm not sure whether that had anything to do with Catholicism, but by the end, I was almost converted... Then came Loveless.

Just so you know about our competition at the time, in the 2000s, Our Lady's nemesis, Megadocs, was in trouble. It was discovered they had been performing heart catherization on every patient that came through the door complaining of chest pain. A Heart Cath is an invasive procedure, so think of it like if you went in for a massage and they gave you a colonic, even though you were a vegan who hadn't eaten in ten days. Oh, and you'd later be billed five grand for the colonic. In addition to this unfun ordeal, many patients found to have very little, if any at all, blockage were then treated to heart stents, costing between $11,000 and $41,000.00, to open the clogged but not really clogged heart vessel.

The scheme was rumored to be the brainchild of the now-disgraced, once renowned cardiac surgeon for whom the 12-story cardiothoracic addition was named. Also rumored to be involved was the villainous, unlikeable CEO, Dirk Wayward. After fines and humiliation, Megadocs decided the best road to recovery would be eliminating 400 jobs, mostly basic staffers to middle management. The surgeon went to jail, but Dirk Wayward remained at the top.

With Megadocs' bad press, Our Lady was continually voted the best hospital in the area, the best place to receive care. We were so proud! This went on for years. Megadocs also lost the ability to do business with any patients using

Medicaid. Losing market share may not have translated into a loss of payment; this was when the cost of treatment for Medicaid far exceeded the reimbursement. Our Lady, already "not for profit" and barely making ends meet, became the only place the poor and marginalized could get care.

Dirk Wayward eventually took a massive retirement package. With nationally reported fraud, mismanagement, and lawsuits nearing 40 million dollars, he quietly slunk away, replaced by the most politically correct figure Megadocs could conjure. I made up in my mind I never wanted to work for such a corrupt organization.

When Love Hospital Systems bought Our Lady in 2018, we, the employees, saw them as an answer to prayer. Most hospitals were merging or were predicted not to survive unless they did merge. Love was a massive healthcare network comprised of 70 facilities along the East Coast and Midwest. We were told this was a "merger," not a "takeover." The cash infusion from Love could allow Our Lady to continue providing great care. The mission would continue. The only change would be cheaper insurance! Power in numbers! Bigger and better!

Love was going to give us some tough love. We had only made a million dollars a year. This, we were told, was not profitable.

"But I thought we were not for profit?" many employees asked.

"You don't understand how it works," Love told us all.

We really didn't understand it all because Love was downtown trying to buy Megadocs, too, even though it was at least 40 million in debt. But Megadocs was locally controlled, and they were a powerful bunch of old-money Kentucky boys. My money was on those Kentucky boys.

November 2018, one week before Thanksgiving. Love executives descended upon Our Lady and eliminated 150 jobs in one day. There was no warning. There was no advance notice to managers. I made the cut but lost one of my dietitians, a sweet, beautiful young girl fresh out of her dietetic internship. Love executives coldly removed the excused workers, security hovering over them as they were escorted off the premises with one cardboard box of memorabilia. There were tears, anger. We were a broken family, and the holidays were upon us.

Love, which we privately called "Loveless," was a ruthless organization. They began to charge fees for Our Lady to be part of their hospital system, moving billing and scheduling remotely to save them money and compensate for the eliminated jobs. For months after the initial purge, many of us sat with our desks packed up… were we next? Then, gradually, personal effects begin to trickle back into place. Finally, we became comfortable with our discomfort.

Our Lady, with low-income clientele, had historically made its way on tiny payments made by many people. Most of the money recouped from individuals was under $500.00. The centralized billing of Loveless Health Systems billed claims under $500.00 only once, if at all. They did not bother to pursue such small amounts! Despite the collection struggles, Our Lady managed to break even by the end of 2019, even showing a miraculous small gain.

On January 2, 2020, I arrived at work at 8:00 am, as usual, walked the two flights to my window-lined office, and unlocked my door to reveal a panoramic view of our newly renovated behavioral health building. This was more than just a hospital. It was a campus, really, with cardiac rehab, a community fitness center, doctor's offices.

The meeting planner popped up at 8:15. Last-minute management meeting, 8:30 am. I'd had a jolt of happiness. Maybe after a year of lean operations, buying our own pens, and contributing our own money to pay for the recruitment of specialty physicians, maybe, just maybe, a raise had been approved! I had quickly organized my daily paperwork and skipped over to the conference room, taking an available seat by Rita, the plant operations manager. I preferred to arrive early to meetings to get one of the leather armchairs, but this fold-out chair would do just fine, as long as the news was good.

Excited murmurs filled the room, managers chatting about the possibilities and comparing stories about the holidays. Then, at 8:30 am sharp, a suit from Loveless took center stage and with no pretense had dropped a bomb: "We brought you all in here today because we've decided to close Our Lady of the River."

An audible gasp went up. Some began to murmur and were silenced by the orator. He explained that it was not financially prudent to keep Our Lady in operation. There had been failed attempts at a "merger" with Megadocs. Of course, we would be provided with career counseling.

I became deaf to his words at that point. Everything was silent as I'd scanned the room, tears streaming down the faces of nurse managers, masks of disbelief and shock on others. Loveless finished the presentation at some point, and we all shuffled out. Some people appeared to be shrieking, holding on to others, but I was strangely calm. I walked pointedly to my office, sat down, and sent my resumé out to the top three employers within an hours' drive. I used company paper and company computers to get the job done.

Details were released about the "shut down," supposedly to be complete by September of the year. But as Loveless swept through the buildings, with their suits and briefcases, a panic ensued. Nurses and doctors, technicians, and IT guys all started to flee. There were five applicants for every open job in the community, so you can imagine my elation when I got an interview with

CapMed. No way was I even applying to MegaDocs! CapMed was an hour away but second to Our Lady, the best paying job prospect for a dietitian. I was going to win it!

Chapter 3: Brad *Pit*

When I first moved back to the Tri-State, I had more things to do than I had time to do them, with work and two kids and fixing up an old house. Then I was dumb enough to try raising goats for a while because the general lay knowledge is that they will keep your grass cut down for you, but it really doesn't work out so great. Those things could escape from Alcatraz, and then they'd run a mile and be out in the road, jumping on people's cars, whatever. If they got diarrhea, they could be dead in 24 hours. They took Pepto-Bismol just like people. It had all been too much, so a goat farmer took them, and I had to start mowing about seven acres of uneven grass on top of all my other chores.

To clarify, the farm was hundreds of acres, but I was only mowing around the house and the barns to keep down the mice and snakes. That's when it hit me: I've got all this property, so why don't I use it to my advantage? I was thinking about the possibilities when I happened to be at the local convenience store-beer joint-pizza place and overheard some folks talking about "Brad (short for Bradbury; his mom was a big science fiction fan) Pit is coming back." Brad Pit—Pit with one "t"—is a local boy. He looked nothing like Brad Pitt (with two "t's") but was also handsome. Brad left the area to play baseball, settling in Florida for a few years after, and then, apparently, intended to return and coach the local high school team.

I didn't know Brad personally—he was three years younger than me in school—but I knew coaches all too well, having been taught valuable life lessons by the one to whom I'd been married. So, while I wasn't in the market for a boyfriend, I was in the market for a renter. I had eased into the conversation and, in doing so, was recognized by one of the men.

"Jolene? What're you doin' back here? I ain't seen you in a coon's age, girl!" He would give my contact information to Brad, who was looking for someplace to settle in. That night, I got a call.

"So, Bud tells me you've got someplace to rent," Brad relayed.

"Kind of," I confessed, "it's actually more of just property, free natural gas, and well water hook-up if you want to pull something in there for now. You see, I was thinking that would give you time to look around and see where you really want to live, without signing a lease or anything."

"Okay, but what do I pay you? Do you have a trailer, or how's this go?" he asked, confused.

"No, I don't have anything but the land, the gas, and the water. I guess I didn't think this through. I just thought maybe you would be willing to trade helping me, like mowing grass once a week here or something. I don't know."

There was a long pause on the other end of the line. Then he said, "I remember you from school, you know."

I answered, "How's that? I'm way older than you."

Flirting, he said, "I always knew about the pretty girls."

Oh, lordy, here we go, I thought. *Do men never grow up?*

"Listen," I said, "I'm way past all that kinda stuff, I've got two kids, I'm going through a divorce, I ain't looking like I used to. It's a lot. If you don't want to live out here, that's fine, but that's all this is, a living arrangement."

Chapter 4: CapMed

Every dietitian in every crappy, low-wage job wanted to work for CapMed, but nobody really knew any of the dietitians that worked for CapMed. It was like they went there and never came back out again. We had all heard of the amazing pay and benefits that far exceeded what the surrounding hospitals could provide.

The possible sticking point with my shot at the open CapMed job was that I had turned down a job at CapMed just a year prior. This was following the layoffs after Our Lady fell mercy to Loveless. I had interviewed for an open position, had been offered the position, then declined. Why? I had loved Our Lady so much, and my coworkers were my family and friends. The campus was like home to me. The only way I could leave her was if it were over-really over-and now it was. I had heard of people being blackballed for declining offers from CapMed. I was elated when the Nutrition Director saw fit to give me a second chance. It wasn't a guaranteed position, only an interview. Every last minute I spent at the dying Loveless was used to burnish my interviewing skills in preparation for the battle ahead.

A "Type A" queen, I was overprepared for that interview. I had responses for any possible question or combination of questions that might be asked. I was the best candidate in the country, and I was going to sell it that day.

Driving into West Virginia practically required passage by land, air, and sea. I had to detour twice to avoid flooding. A fallen tree thwarted one detour. Swerving to miss deer, rumbling over rickety wooden bridges, and winding through acres of national forest roads kept my mind alert. There was mist between the hills and the hollows, obstructing the mountain tops. Crossing the state line as the sun rose, steam floated up off the Ohio River, and barges made their way downstream. A lotto billboard advertised Mega Millions and Powerball. There was a long stretch of seedy 24-hour gaming /Keno "coffee shops," adult bookstores, "gentlemen's clubs," and cash advance storefronts dotting the final riverfront miles as I closed in on my destination.

Approaching from the highway, I could see that the building was a sprawling, neoclassical beauty. Deer, raccoons, and other creatures roamed the property, which employed its own animal containment specialist. A long, paved drive led to remote parking areas and walking trails. Such a peaceful location compared to the sad establishments in the valley below. I had given myself an hour and a half to get there, so with minutes to spare, I reviewed my interview notes in the car and said a prayer before swinging open my door.

"If you're on time, you're late!" my mom always told me, "Make sure you have time to change a flat tire if need be."

My black, designer mid-heel shoes hit the pavement as I stood, smoothing my pressed interview suit. Then, grabbing the leather briefcase, which contained eight embossed folders full of my resumé and certifications, I headed toward the office of Mrs. Prudence Townsend, Nutrition Director.

As I walked, I remembered a girl who had interviewed, wearing yoga pants and flip-flops, for a job in my department at Our Lady. Before I could even ask her the first question, she started with, "When I was driving in here this morning, I think I didn't realize just how small this town is... like, I don't know if I could live here..." Which was good, because there was not a chance she was going to be hired.

Most dietitians' offices aren't very impressive. This was no exception (Formica furniture, Berber carpeting, no windows) so the décor wasn't depressing to me. On the other hand, the untidy appearance of the workers I encountered was depressing and off-putting. The dress code at CapMed seemed non-existent. The personal hygiene also seemed non-existent.

I had never before seen a secretary like this, with bedraggled, greasy hair, wearing a patterned leggings-top combo with faux Birkenstocks exposing unkempt feet. The leggings hung loosely, puddled fabric on her bony frame. Hair, mid-length and dark, parted directly down the middle and gave no clue to her age. She wore no makeup, although she desperately needed it. I estimated she was between 45 and 65 years old and made an instant decision to be kind to her because she was a pitiful creature, indeed.

There was once a time when I, too, was the ugly duckling.

Chapter 5: Swansong

Long after I'd lost the gift of music to serpent-induced motor coordination issues, I lost my baby-faced cuteness, too. My pre-teen life was a seemingly continual series of confidence destruction and unsolicited self-mortification. I had weight gain without growth in stature, oily skin and acne, and a meek personality. My teeth were gapped in front, and one turned slightly askew. My hair was mousy blonde, limp and lifeless. With little money for clothing, my wardrobe could not elevate the situation.

I remember being a young girl, doing cartwheels in the front yard, dreaming that someone important would pass by and recognize my brilliance. They would put me on TV, and I'd become a famous child star. The shoes I loved in the JCPenney Christmas catalog? I'd have a pair in every color. Of course, it never happened, but I was a Pisces, and I had big dreams.

Many kids were in tight financial situations in Appalachia and just getting by. I hadn't given poverty much thought, then, because most of us were wearing hand-me-downs or shopping at yard sales. It wasn't until I was an adult and moved away when I saw us the way the rest of the country sees us. I watched an episode of American Idol, the charity episode, where they are usually in some African village somewhere, and they were IN EASTERN KENTUCKY. So, I started calling all my (then) friends where I lived (in California) and said, "Are you watching this??" And they would all give me a similar answer, something on a variation of "I know, it's so sad that people would live like that, isn't it?" That's when I knew I had to get back home, just had to pack up and go. Why was I staying in such a superficial place?

Back in the early '80s, I was tortured by my appearance. There was a mean bully on my school bus named Sarah Ringer, whose family people said worshipped Satan. They didn't go to church anywhere and lived at the mouth of a long, dark hollow. Within earshot of me, she would ask my sister, "How's your brother doing?" There were only us two siblings. Once as I climbed onto the bus and made my way down the narrow rubber pathway for seat selection, Sarah, ear-to-ear welcoming smile, waved me her way. My naïve heart filled with joy at the prospect of a foe-turned-friend. As I bent to sit, a sharp, quick pain sent me straight back up… Sarah was holding a stick pin. "Just kidding!!" she said. In the backseat of the bus, Doug Maynard was self-piercing his ear with a safety pin.

An 8th-grade history teacher once called me to the board to write an answer, then mocked my lumbering stride all the way up the aisle: "da-dump, da-dump, da-dump, da-dump, da-dump, da-da-da-da-dump-da-dump." I could feel my face redden with embarrassment, of course. There were run-of-the-mill mean girls, too. Good friends became teen queens over the summer, then forgot your name in the fall.

Over the summer, my body started stretching out all that stored-up fat and using all that extra oil to make my hair shiny when I snuck and used household bleach on it. Long-dormant cheekbones emerged, high with hollows below. I had a Coppertone tan and one single tube of baby pink lipstick. Every morning all summer long, I'd rise up to a small portion of oats or fruit followed by an hour-long sweaty session of VHS-led aerobics.

Like Abraham Lincoln failing to get elected over and over, yet one day becoming president, all the indignities of being an ugly duckling would drastically shape my behavior as a swan. I had a guy tell me once, upon hearing my history as a pariah, "That explains a lot because girls that look like you are usually stuck-up snobs."

Chapter 6: The Gift

That pitiful secretary? Her name was Patricia Sweets. Only she was not a secretary. She was the manager of dietitians. Yes. I wasn't sure I'd won the day. I seemed extremely overqualified. Ms. Sweets kept making comments like, "But I just think you might get bored here." The "big" boss, Mrs. Townsend ("Call me Prudence"), seemed nonchalant about the whole interview, really, mostly seeming impressed by my accomplishments at Our Lady.

"I can't believe you got coverage for that! We've been trying for months," she said. "I want to talk to you more. Maybe you can help us." Prudence laughed at my jokes. Prudence was in my corner.

I knew there were certain red flags to look for in interviews, signs you don't want to work at the place with whom you are interviewing. At CapMed, there were conflicting answers about workplace morale, benefits, and even pay, but the job market was optionless, and I wanted money and benefits. So, red flags flying, I moved forward.

There was a spin-off Q&A with other staffers, including a nurse, yet ANOTHER manager, Georgia, and the dietitian awaiting the full-time helper. Her name was Jessica Miller. I could tell Jessica was not amused. Her body language gave off a borderline angry tone, and she had just argued with this manager, Georgia, about the last interviewed candidate. Georgia wanted to hire that interviewee, but Jessica fought against the choice. She said the person hadn't even passed the exam to become a dietitian yet, and the open job demanded an experienced, seasoned dietitian.... THAT is when I knew I would get the job. I waited in the lobby, two hallways away, while their arguing intensified. THIS is when I need to tell you

27

something about myself. When the Lord took away one gift, He gave me another.

Call it The Gift. Call it The Sight. I didn't have The Sight until I got pregnant with my son. In a dream, I saw him, and the following day told his father the baby would have red hair. He did. After his birth, I didn't experience the joy of my child. I didn't experience any happy thoughts at all.

We had been attending a mega-church at the time, where medication was strongly discouraged, considered a sign of weakness or lack of faith. I spiraled into a depression that would nearly become madness through a mixture of arcane beliefs and misguided Biblical interpretations. Irina, the Russian-born wife of a church pastor, had come to call and bring vegan lunch offerings, unannounced. In a haggard mess of nerves and matted hair, I hid under my dining room table while she rang the doorbell and knocked on a variety of windows. The baby began to cry. I was like a feral animal, trapped, praying her away. Then, after what seemed like hours, she was gone.

My then-husband, fed-up more than concerned, took me back to the obstetrician, who immediately put me on antidepressants for three months, solving the problem and creating peaceful living conditions. I know now that the medication also blocked my ability to See all the things that may have been revealed to me at that time... and for that, I am thankful. There is no way I could have handled the information then. God has His timing (*Habakkuk 2:3 "For still, the vision awaits its appointed time…"*).

As soon as the medication was cleared from my system and the baby was sleeping through the night, I began to reclaim my life and part-time work and fitness, eating out, and all the good things. I would occasionally take the baby and drop by my husband's office space, but he was primarily mobile, with house calls and cross-country flights throughout the week.

One rare weekday we met for lunch at a bistro with outdoor seating, and I remember every detail of the cushions of those seats: off-white, with cornflower-blue leaves and flowers scrolling up and over, tied to pale wicker bases with perfect bows. I admired this attention to detail when I saw her legs, then her body, interrupting our lunch. "A friend." We shook hands, and when we did, I SAW.

I would shake many hands over the next few years, would touch many shoulders. Sometimes, the Sight would flood into me; other times, I wouldn't See at all. I paid a private detective to try and back up my allegations. Unfortunately, as you've already been told, they found a lot more than just cheating in the marriage.

Chapter 7: Of the Devil

*Acts 16:16- "...a certain damsel possessed with a
spirit of divination met us, which brought her
masters much gain by soothsaying...."*

Growing up in any old Appalachian country church before
1990, you would have some fundamental commonalities
regardless of denomination. Hymnbooks including "The
Old Rugged Cross" and "Just as I Am" were the standard.
The Holy Trinity includes God the Father, Jesus the Son,
and Holy Spirit.

Practices diverged where "gifts" were concerned.
Some believed The Spirit could still descend upon a
person, filling a person with an indecipherable voice
(speaking in tongues) to anyone but the person being
blessed as an interpreter at the time. Some churches took
literally passages about drinking poison and handling
serpents without injury. Other churches believed those
gifts were sent to earth for only a specified period long ago
called Pentecost, and nobody had those types of gifts
anymore.

The latter type of church (no more big gifts) believed
that everything could be important. We all played a role in
God's kingdom. Some people sing, some preach, and
some teach, some sweep the floors, some attend and listen,
but everybody can help in some small way. But one thing
all the churches believed was definitely not a gift from the
Lord? Telling the future, or "soothsaying." Only God
knew the future. So, if you were getting a message about
it, it wasn't coming from God. It was coming from
DEMONS! The Bible says we are surrounded by spirits,
which is terrifying to me, so I don't like to think about it.

The gift of Prophecy was different than soothsaying, but until I was an older woman, I didn't know it, so I kept my Gift of Sight to myself. I didn't want people to think I was some Hell-bent soothsayer. When you prophesy, you just deliver a message, and those messages I had delivered? They were from the RIGHT NOW (He was already cheating. The baby was in my womb but already had red hair. The person was calling me on the phone, so it was going to ring any second...)

> Micah 5:12 *"And I will cut off witchcrafts out of thine hand; and thou shalt have no more soothsayers...."*

Chapter 8: Pregame Training

Every time you start a new hospital job, you have orientation for at least a day or two. I was pleased to hear that orientation would last a whole week with CapMed because I wanted to make sure I understood everything. In my interviews, my main emphasis was that I was interviewing them, too. Finding my new work family and staying until retirement were my goals. What they got in return was the best, most knowledgeable dietitian for the job.

The long orientation didn't come to pass, though. COVID-19 was just beginning to change the landscape. New employees were sent away on day two to report to the department in which they would be working. Day one consisted of one human resources rep, dressed in the equivalent of a HazMat suit, showing recorded segments about handwashing and privacy. There was a pre-recorded speech of the CapMed President, an elderly gentleman, welcoming everyone and extolling the core values and mission.

"Due to the recent COVID-19 problem, this is the first time we are trying to do this orientation differently. Everyone who doesn't work with patients is just working from home, so here are some numbers to call if you can't figure out how to do something…. Here are the websites to sign up for insurance and all that…."

Meanwhile, the paperwork we were provided was clearly copied from a previous orientee ("Matt Davis") because his signature was already on all the documents. We were told to "Wite-Out" Mr. Davis, add our own information, and just "send it back in later." Agreeing that

COVID should be taken seriously, I appreciated the distancing and masks, but the first impression was that this place was a disorganized mess.

One girl literally quit and walked out before the day was even done: "Matt Davis is my cousin, and you all know what you're doing. I'm calling a lawyer." She packed up her notebook, pens, and crossbody bag, and she was out the door.

Nobody spoke, and a full sixty seconds of silence filled the air until the HR guy, without missing a beat, said, "So take some Wite-Out...."

Day two, for me, meant reporting to Miss Sweets. Miss Sweets was to train me on all my job duties at CapMed. When I arrived that Tuesday afternoon, Sweets "wasn't ready" and sent me home, with pay, for the rest of the day.

"I thought you would be in there for a couple of weeks," she stated, apparently unaware that orientation had been modified. It looked like she had Facebook pulled up on her work computer, so when I got to the parking lot, I pulled up the app on my phone and found her account. We weren't friends, and I didn't want to raise any red flags, so I just tucked the information away.

I sat in my car for a few minutes, then decided to look at all the paperwork provided by the HR rep the day before and realized I had a few questions. Wandering down the deserted corridor, I remembered being told that non-essential workers were working remotely. There was one open door as I neared the administrative offices: Human Resources Director. It was refreshing to see a human in the flesh. Her name was Donna, and she helped me fill out the forms and even provided her business card as I thanked her and rose to go. The second the card hit my palm, I started to See parts of her private life that weren't so nice, but I struggled to focus on the professional side of things. Everyone did things in private. I didn't want to know this woman's business. Why would it matter to me?

Come Wednesday, I tried to dress down, choosing a generic wrap dress with flats. I didn't want to widen the gap between Miss Sweets and myself any further by showcasing my wardrobe. Besides, any time I dropped my daughter off at my mom's place wearing anything from The Mall or "snooty stores," I'd get the "don't get above your raisin'" talk. The older I got, the worse my feet hurt at the end of each day if I wore heels, anyway.

Wednesday started with a "tour" of sorts, unlike any I had experienced with past employers. Miss Sweets took apple turnovers from patient trays and shoved them into her chapped mouth as we strolled, free of masks and hair nets, through the kitchen. She stopped for awkward small talk with a prep cook who seemed confused by the visit. Although I believed she was trying to convey "I am liked, respected, and in control," she presented as a buffoon acting out a painfully obvious power flex.

Six hours and no training later, I was suffering from an extreme case of TMI (too much information.) The Story of Sweets was unfolding. And while it was a poor, poor, pitiful tale, it was exacerbated by Miss Sweets herself. I'd been told way more than I needed to know, and it made me dislike rather than pity her. I had little respect for someone who relished confiding their woes in others but never initiated the readily available tools that could remedy those very woes.

To be fair, everybody handles life's problems differently. Myers Briggs testing changed my life and helped me see different perspectives, but I also know that not everybody is qualified for every job. You can't turn Michael Jackson into Michael Jordan.

At the end of the 8-hour day, I made my way out to my car and sat in the front seat, thinking about what had just happened. I had just gotten paid a dietitian's salary for a day's work as a psychotherapist... not an even trade.

Tomorrow would be better, I told myself. The training would happen.

Thursday and Friday were two of the longest days of my life. Traveling a different route to this hospital than to my last, my coming and going was registered by a large, aggressive Great Pyrenees-Saint Bernard mix I began referring to as "Cujo." A car-chaser by nature, the beast would hide in the deep roadside ditch, obscured by weeds, exploding out of the cover at the very moment of my passing. On Thursday morning, he had leaped straight out of his moat, slamming his total weight into the driver's side door and scaring the life out of me. I just wanted to learn my job that day, preferably under the tutelage of someone other than Miss Sweets.

"Be nice, be nice, be nice...." My internal conversation was keeping me stable. It was hour two of the one-sided therapy/hostage situation they called training, and I wanted to scream.

Basically, three things were happening that day. One: Miss Sweets was lamenting every sad event or slight she'd ever perceived had happened. Two: I'd responded to each with an adequate, well-placed "Oh, no" or "Mmmm" although my social battery had died hours prior, and Three: My brain had its own internal witty retort, the only thing keeping me sane. I just did not like this woman, and there was no logical reason other than my strong intuition that she was collecting a paycheck she didn't deserve. What follows is a brief sampling of the maddening training day:

Miss Sweets started complaining about what she considered an unfair childhood: "My dad had to work in the mines... we didn't see him much. He made too much money for me to get help with payment for school, yet a bunch of other people got help!"

You knew him, though! He had a job, though! Can we stop talking about fathers, please? Get over yourself!

She would then begin to sing her own praises: "I had to work my way up around here and put myself through college."

You and everyone else here. I can't stand another minute with you, you ungrateful woman.

Her opinions of men and dating were explored: "In my opinion, all men are cheaters, and I do not want that in my life."

Why is this relevant to my job?

In addition to her complaints about the males of our species, she made known that Prudence had little respect for her: "The boss here treats me like I don't know what I'm doing!"

Why would you tell this to a new hire? I can see her point.

And she even took the time to blame the public education system for any perceived shortcomings: "I can't do most math, and it's because I never had good teachers, so I can't do some of the dietitian stuff. That's not my fault."

Why would you tell anyone this? How did you get this job?

Although she had the time to talk to me for days about irrelevant topics, she added: "I'm just so busy all the time! This job has me in meetings all day! People don't understand what I go through."

Nobody would understand what I'm going through.

Finally, my secretly-held belief that she knew nothing about nutrition was confirmed with her statements at lunchtime: "Have you tried the keto diet? Dr. Oz says…".

KILL ME NOW!

The talk inside my mind would get like this sometimes, so constant a narrative it would practically drown out the reality around me. It didn't really matter in this instance because Sweets wasn't looking for a response. She just talked constantly about herself, and no feedback was necessary. But long after I left the building, as I drove in my car, my mind raced, and I daydreamed about the disorganization of CapMed and Miss Sweet's incompetence, and although the drive was an hour, I was already home and unsure how I had gotten there.

"So, Marina's sister's husband had a daughter when he met her, and she had some health issues. She wound up in the hospital with some things, and we were all a-prayin' for her...". "And so, I've been sayin' about my house; it's ancient and in need of *so many* repairs, and I just don't know if I can afford them all and...".

I was into my (hopefully) last day (Friday) of the personal history not only of Miss Sweets but also Miss Sweets' family and people she once knew. No topic was off-limits, and even though Sweets knew nothing about my personal life, she used her bully pulpit to extol the virtues of the Republican party, Southern Baptists, and perms while expressing disdain for "liberals," "those trans people," and cheaters. "But, of course, you can't tell anybody your opinions at work," she confided in me.

That morning on my way in, I noticed I was still the best-dressed person in the facility, although I'd dropped another level to sub-business casual polo-shirt/khaki pants-attire. Anything goes here: "Jorts" (jean shorts), tights, open-toed shoes on the medical units! The dress code could best have been described as early nineties spring-summer Sears catalog.

I tried all day to contain my emotions while internally my rage against this woman, Miss Sweets, contended with my will to survive and keep the job. Wrestling with my quickly formed negative feelings as the day concluded, I collected my notes on the nothing I'd learned. Was I just jealous that this inept woman had a job that I could do so much better? I was miffed that anyone who claimed to be a church-going Christian would collect money for a job they were not performing well. Sweets finally handed me a job description I should have been given on day one. As the document passed between our hands, a warning jolted into me, like a flashing revelation of her potential for evil. All the things I'd been thinking were true.

I was thanking the same God she claimed to believe in that I'd be released to my job the following Monday morning, even though I wasn't prepared at all. I knew nobody and nothing, only to show up to room N-73 at 8:00 am, which I would do fifteen minutes early ("If you're on time, you're late," again, per Mom.) Monday would kick off my introduction to a cast of characters in a big drama that would unfold over the following year, changing my life and plans forever.

Chapter 9: From Whence We Came

"Why would you move back here?" or "Why would you want to move out *there* in the first place?" were really the only two responses from the people of my area when they heard I had lived in California. In reality, both places had pros and cons. But this part of Appalachia had taken some hits over time. The steel mills and coal mines were being phased out, and we were #1 for drug addiction. We were #1 for obesity back in the early 2000s. There were documentaries made about us and our troubles.

This land was home to one of the worst tragedies in US college sports (1970 plane crash of Marshall University football team), cover-ups and conspiracies (big chemical companies polluting the water with carcinogens), and big pharma flooding Oxycontin to an area they knew had work-related injuries aplenty. If we were known at all nationally, it was for sadness and despair. One Eastern Kentucky attorney almost got away with the biggest Social Security/disability rip-off ever committed, earning himself an *American Greed* episode and a prison cell. Then, there were *The Wild and Wonderful Whites of West Virginia* with their Hillbilly mating call, the sound of a rattling pill bottle.

Even on a micro-level, there were everyday problems in Appalachia to which urban dwellers could not relate. There were chicken-borne, bat-borne, and tick-borne diseases you could contract that could end with you having a glass eye, a chronic debilitating illness, or a meat allergy. This stuff can't be made up!

My son had decided to go back to California after graduating from high school. But, unlike the protagonist of *Hillbilly Elegy,* he hated his visits to Kentucky, preferring concrete to conifers.

"Mom, why do you want to stay in such a dead-end place? All the businesses are shutting down, the people on drugs??" he pleaded.

Answering a question with a question, I'd asked, "What if all the good people left those areas? Somebody who cares needs to stay or go in and try to make a difference."

This part of Appalachia (eastern Kentucky, western West Virginia, and southern Ohio) is called "The Tri-State" locally. And yes, southern Ohio is VERY Appalachian. Not all Ohio is flat and urban, with cornfields on the outskirts. There are comically gerrymandered maps that include southern Ohio as part of West Virginia. Deer hunting is big in this part of the state. Pick-up trucks and tractors are commonly seen on the roads, and Amish buggies travel the more remote locations. There are a few small towns in that rural "Tri-State" section of Ohio, but the bigger towns—the shopping, the hospitals, the jobs—are in Kentucky and West Virginia.

Kentuckians and West Virginians say Ohioans can't drive, don't use turning signals. Ohioans end sentences with prepositions: "Where is the tape at?" Ohioans say the Kentuckians and West Virginians have one leg shorter than the other from standing on the sides of hills. Kentuckians and West Virginians both see each other as hillbillies in some leftover Hatfield-McCoy-style pride (less deadly, of course.) Dwellers from these parts of all three states make fun of one another, but if someone from anywhere else dares utter a negative word about us, we become a collective "US," united, and "Them are fightin' words."

We have meth and heroin, but there are stories behind it all. The rest of the country doesn't seem to care that many of these addicts started as injured miners, providing the fuel this country once ran on, or injured steelworkers responsible for making the very chassis of the cars people drive or skeletons of the buildings in which they live. There is beauty in the pain and beauty in the sadness, and the rivers and the woods and the mountains are home to us all.

It would eventually be revealed in the West Virginia opioid trial against big pharma that company executives had called addicted Appalachians "pillbillies" and referred to Kentucky as "OxyContinville." Drugs meant to ease people's pain, directed by sadists. Why were people in power who shouldn't be?

Chapter 10: Daisy and the Basic Training

Settling in at CapMed was rough because the people with actual jobs had to do their jobs while helping me learn mine, too. I was anxious to learn my job because of personal achievement and the desire to help unburden the overworked compatriots. Jessica was the other hospital dietitian. If she had seemed irritated in my interview, she seemed outright hostile to the fact that I had arrived in the office unprepared to see patients. Too busy to bother with my questions, she commanded Daisy to train me.

Daisy was a sweet 30-something diet clerk with a family at home. Before the big school consolidation, she had gone to high school right down the road and now lived beside her parents on a dirt road off Goose Creek. She went to community college for a quarter before becoming pregnant with her first child, then found work at CapMed and never went back. The kind of religious person who makes you want to find religion, she rarely talked about her beliefs but simply led by example. Anyone could tell she was Pentecostal because she was a "skirt lady" and never cut her hair or wore makeup.

Daisy talked really slowly and told stories about her children and 4-H and gardening and cooking and farming that sometimes would veer off into one another and last for longer than was possible to listen to at work. Also, regardless of the food item foraged, harvested, or hunted, she could create a culinary masterpiece worthy of praise to share with Jessica and me.

"You all, I made some cushaw muffins if you want any." "Well, my mom gave me some of these wild ramps, and so I brought some in I cooked." "I got some paw paw bread here."

"Diet Clerk" was Daisy's official job title, and the duties included everything from helping dietitians to helping kitchen staff.

"Miss Sweets used to work in here, too," Daisy confided. "She was a Diet Clerk before she got picked to manage."

"But weren't you here longer?" I asked.

"Yeah, but they picked her for it," stated Daisy, accepting her fate.

When basic daily expectations were established for me by the girls, I had help with the process via the Big Green Bible, an ancient binder with Times New Roman-font printouts (and some hand-written!) of directions for daily tasks that hadn't been updated since 1994. Ends up, the dietitians were doing the same thing they were doing back in '94. Coming from a world of "Best Practice," this laissez-faire attitude toward changing with the times blew my mind, and I started asking questions. Lots of questions. And that's when they all started telling me lots of things.

It would take a full two months to learn my job due to the slow pace of training and mass exodus of all things non-clinical because of COVID. In addition, the job was way more cumbersome than it needed to be, full of bureaucracy and double documentation. I didn't get access to the computer system for weeks because Sweets kept incorrectly filling out the access form. I finally intervened, completing the form, her only task a signature.

She seemed grateful for the help: "I'm just so busy! And I've gotta work from home some now, what with my house messin' up and all!"

The Big Green Bible was at least seven years behind best practice, and it was driving me crazy. There was no contingency plan for short staffing. If somebody called off, the person left behind was expected to do the job of two. Management didn't appreciate overachievement in clinical areas but had a keen eye for perceived slights related to food service. Outlandish at it may seem, the clinical dietitians, who had nothing to do with food preparation or delivery, fielded calls from angry patients and were imposed upon by Sweets to serve as the ambassadors of the kitchen, to explain why trays were late or food was cold. All this atop a clinical caseload of mental health patients, surgical patients, and patients receiving feedings via gastric tubes or intravenous routes.

I brought out my old nutrition screening policy from Our Lady and formatted it to fit CapMed, presenting it to Miss Sweets at the end of May. She seemed impressed with my initiative and fresh set of eyes. Sweets confided that she had never written a policy before, which was why the policies never changed. Our Lady had required policy revisions every two years, so this was shocking to me, and I asked if CapMed didn't have any requirement for revision. Sweets didn't know. She would "see about" getting the policy revised.

In my free time, I would read all the documents I could find in the online file folder our department had posted. I wanted to try and learn all the things I had missed due to having an irregular orientation and training. Unfortunately, this was the time I finally found the full policy and procedure manual, and there was no tube feeding policy, which was not acceptable for a clinical dietetics department.

So, one Tuesday afternoon, I found a CapMed template and wrote the tube feeding policy using national guidelines. I had spoken with the Chief of Surgery and had incorporated his demands into the mix. Miss Sweets didn't know how to do her job, but this had to be taken care of, so I would present it to her. A win-win situation. The brilliant Stephen Covey would have been proud! After I finalized the document, I sent it to Sweets with a "sweet" sentiment and cc'd Prudence and the Chief of Surgery. I went home Friday evening, happy we would soon have a policy, but still hearing no response from management.

The following week, I was told on Tuesday I had been exposed to COVID and had to be tested. I was sent home. The testing result was supposed to be back within three days, but I'd heard nothing by Friday. I called in, but Sweets and Prudence didn't take my calls. Nobody called me back. Monday morning, I called in. Four days without pay was a lot. Again, nobody would take my call or call me back. I drove in, went to the office, and had Daisy call Sweets, who picked up immediately. Daisy asked about the test. It had come back negative on Friday.

Chapter 11: Campfire Stories

Jessica still hadn't warmed to me. It was hard to warm to anything in the dungeon we called an office. Wedged between the foodservice delivery dock and the morgue, we had to run space heaters to exhaustion. There was a sliver of a window through which we could view hearses coming and going, loading COVID bodies over and over throughout the days. In addition, my cubicle was very dim. I was still sitting in the dark despite continually asking Sweets for a lightbulb for the past two months.

"Things take time at CapMed," was her response that week. She had already gone through: "I've ordered it," "That bulb was a special order," "They don't make those bulbs anymore," and "I have to order a new light fixture, and the person to order from is out for two weeks."

So, I had to wait until next month to see. What was up with this woman?

I'd met other staffers who served in areas outside our realm (bariatric, cardiac rehab, outpatient dialysis clinic, home health) and in other disciplines managed by our department (speech therapy and occupational therapy.) Unique to CapMed, these two services fell under Nutrition Department control because 1) speech therapists have to order thickener and we provide that, then have to order the diets they want and 2) occupational therapists have to have "adaptive equipment" like special forks and plates in the hospital, and we are in charge of that.

One by one, they pulled me aside to imbue similar words of warning: "Watch out for Sweets." There were other variations on this theme: "She's an idiot, but she's got something on someone." "She somehow got that job and does nothing, and we all suffer for it, but the more you do to make things better, the worse it will be for you." Even "She's never going to like you because you are pretty, and you were a manager, so you'll know things aren't right here."

Staying out of the drama was my preferred scenario, but a team would likely need to be chosen according to these ladies. You were either for managers or against them. I sensed some distrust from the staffers toward my wanting to maintain neutrality, but deep down, I believed there had to be some hypersensitivity on their parts. This was, after all, a stable job in an unstable market and less demanding than many. But I kept these thoughts to myself.

"I think I may have misstepped," I said, explaining how I had written the policies.

"Ha! I wrote those same policies ten years ago," bemused the veteran dietitian of our group, "and here we are, still waiting. My advice? Just do your job and go home. Collect your money. Detach from what you know is right. And if you are like me and you can't do that, wait until something comes open in a different division and get out of here. But don't do anything extra, trust me!!"

Following a staff meeting, the group conversed in the office that day, voices lowered to avoid detection (everyone seemed ridiculously paranoid at CapMed), recounting personal stories of abuse.

"Annie" was reprimanded for refusing to work with a pedophile. She was threatened with demotion and moved to a different location. Soon after her move, the law came in and arrested the pedophile AT WORK... he was doing that stuff on his work computer. Annie never even got a "Sorry." When she applied for a management training program for up-and-comers, she was passed over for a new hire that sat around listening to all Sweets' stories. Annie ended up leaving the medical field altogether, taking a job with the local news. She told everybody the stress of the newsroom was nothing compared with CapMed.

A few years back, a beautiful girl in the kitchen was being stalked by a male employee. When she complained, Sweets asked her if she had been "leading him on." He was told to stop bothering her. That was the "solution." Nobody knows what happened to the beauty, but the perpetrator still worked at CapMed. The stalker was later revealed to be a personal friend of the Sweets family.

During an impromptu meeting, with Daisy looking on, "Dietitian X" asked Miss Sweets a question. Miss Sweets didn't answer, so Dietitian X asked again. Finally, Miss Sweets stormed out, "writing up" the dietitian, citing disrespect. The only thing that saved Dietitian X was that she told them Daisy had been within earshot. Daisy, honest as always, refused to sign Sweets' supporting document, and the reprimand was thrown out.

"Don't ever question anything Sweets says!" they warned, "She will make something up about you."

Sweets disliked "Dietitian Y" and began a campaign to have her fired. An "unnamed individual" was said to have seen Dietitian Y leave the facility for two hours on company time. She had to provide witnesses from that day, three months prior, to defend herself against the false claim, and for months after she kept time-stamped proof of her activities, including her comings and goings. Sweets would be lurking by her office door when she arrived each morning, ready to explode at even a moment's tardiness. Dietitian Y ended up eating lunch at her desk, in front of the computer each day, because Sweets would march up and down the outer hallway with a clipboard making notes from 11:00 to noon, and Dietitian Y was sure her lunch break was being monitored.

"When you are the victim of her dislike, she will do anything she can to hurt you. Until she moves on to the next victim." All the girls confirmed Miss Sweets' pattern.

When it was "Dietitian Z's" turn to take some abuse, extra work and unimportant projects were thrown on her for months while Sweets and the office brown-noser took long lunches together and schmoozed with the executives. Sweets wouldn't answer her calls and even took some of Brownie's caseload off, placing it on Dietitian Z. Struggling to get finished every day, she finally broke and went to plead with Sweets, only to find Brownie and Sweets had left early to go shopping. In the yearly employee review, Sweets claimed that Dietitian Z was unproductive, slow, and a complainer, but Brownie received a glowing recommendation. Dietitian Z now works as a realtor downtown.

There was always favoritism. A cast of at least two brown-nosers frequented the office of Sweets, hanging out, doing lunch, Facebook friending. A different core group did all the work so these few could receive payment for showing up sometimes, completing the obligatory patient consult once per day, and providing a phone call or e-mail message once a week. If you were a favorite, you could come in late without retribution. You could leave early, set your own hours, work from home any day of the week.

There were also those who had once been victimized. Some had fought, lost, and been broken but stayed. Others had simply left. But nobody won. Nothing was ever done, and nobody knew why.

Every dietitian who had rotated through the inpatient position had experienced both the passive-aggressive devices of Sweets and the outright, uncontrolled hostility of the other manager, Georgia. Sweets was said to connivingly plant the seeds of mistrust and hate into the mind of the disturbed and daft morning manager, Georgia, who would in turn boil to the point of eruption. Georgia had screamed into faces, thrown papers and books, and stormed around with clenched fists.

I was learning about the dynamics of the place and the people's personalities, and what I was learning made me sad. These strong, intelligent, capable dietitians should have been thriving but instead were cowering, micromanaged, and expected to dumb down and suck up.

Chapter 12: Drive Time, Dietitians, and the Things They Despise

The CapMed staffers would all end up asking me where I lived, followed by the same questions: "How long does it take you to get here? How can you stand the drive?" Drive time and dietitians go hand-in-hand because these jobs can be scarce in rural areas. There are few opportunities, and the unprecedented closure of a hospital, expelling not one but four dietitians into an already strained job market means choices have to be made. The choices include packing up and moving to a new location, applying for unemployment, or simply driving an even farther distance.

To some, a forty-minute commute sounds daunting, but from my remote home, EVERYTHING (grocery store, hospital, society in general) was a minimum forty-minute drive in any direction. A county high school was the closest employer, about a twenty-minute drive from the house, but I was no schoolteacher. In a season of burnout, I considered teaching as a career move. Although I possessed a minor in chemistry and a master's degree in human nutrition, I was told that when it came to being a science teacher in the schools, "medical sciences don't count, only 'life sciences.'" This was all despite the school system being in desperate need of science teachers at the time. My organic and biochemistry were not enough.

When I first moved back from California and wasn't yet working full-time, I really enjoyed the peaceful quiet of living so far away from civilization. Other than the one snake snafu early in life, I'd always had a kinship with nature and animals and enjoyed the solitude, too. But, loving nature aside, even the most hardcore outdoorsman will admit that driving to work in snow and ice is no fun. I needed that full-time work for health insurance, though, and you get used to a commute, regardless of the minutes or hours it takes. You zone out, show up at work, and think, "How did I even get here?" And a commute was a must because I had less reliable internet than some third world countries. Health coaching from home was out. Jobs were hard to come by.

I caught on fast that CapMed wasn't the mecca I'd hoped for. Instead, there were days up to entire weeks where a black mood descended upon the staff. "If you want anything done here, learn to do it yourself," was the motto, but occasionally even the long-term employees got sick of bringing in paper and pens from home or trying to scrounge up surgical masks in the age of shortages.

"There's a prison across from my nephew's elementary school. And I hear that they give them masks," declared Jessica's friend, Kate, as she recounted a graduation ceremony she recently attended. She continued and said, "So I guess if you want toilet paper and masks, then just get in jail or something. They probably get free pens, too! It's like on the way there you also pass ALL the billboards for lawyers, you know? I mean, I was so impressed, I wrote them down." She read out the slogans she'd seen along the highway: "Size Matters", "Just because you did it doesn't mean you're guilty", "She doesn't take 'no' for an answer", "Have you been diagnosed with mesothelioma?", "Have you been injured in an accident?", "You may be entitled to compensation", "Free consultation", "We'll even come to you!"

"Man, that's a lot of suing!" exclaimed Daisy.

"So," Jessica commented, "you experienced attorneys and prison and graduation. Anything else interesting?"

"Well," Kate continued again, "the graduation was typical, but even so, it made me a little sad. Not just because my nephew was graduating, but because of the expectation-vs-reality thing. There was the usual slideshow with all the pictures of the kids growing up, with their guns and bows, the fish they caught, kids on horses, kids on four-wheelers. Some weren't done professionally; couldn't afford them, you could tell. Then, as they gave out diplomas to each kid, they told what the plan for that kids' future was, and I just thought that was sad and wrong. Most of those kids can't afford college, or emphasis was never placed on school. Some of 'em come from generations of welfare. The vast majority were just "undecided" or "planning to pursue employment."

Nobody commented. We were all well aware of the probable outcome awaiting many of those kids.

When you look up low-stress jobs or careers that make people happy, you'll often find dietetics as an option. Unfortunately, this was not the case at CapMed. A bad manager can ruin any career path. Particular to all dietitians, even the happy ones, there are a few things many can agree they dislike. At CapMed, a combination of a few old-school doctors, passive-aggressive managers, and our unchanging nutrition policies fed us a daily dose of unhappiness.

"I'm sick and tired of these outdated policies," complained Jessica, "and doctor's not even knowing any better than to consult us for low albumin. It is NOT a good indicator of malnutrition!!"

You probably don't know if you aren't a dietitian, but memes are made about this. Dietitians detest this. An albumin lab value is not an indicator of malnutrition, and to assess patients for it is a grave misuse of time. Sweets continued to ignore my updated policy recommendations, and CapMed continued to operate in the dark ages.

Dietitians also despise some small things non-dietitians do, like spelling dietitian "dietician," with a "c." Again, there are memes about this. Sweets herself, suspected by many of the staffers to be an imposter with a fake degree, spelled her own purported title wrong. With this so-called leadership, things were unlikely to improve.

"Are there annoying and stupid people in the field of dietetics? Yes. But there are also brilliant people in this field, placing feeding tubes and calculating the nutritional needs of the elderly. It's not all about weight loss, people. Sadly, we have ignorance from the top down here," I griped, adding to the general consensus that dietitians were misunderstood and disrespected at CapMed.

To become a registered, licensed dietitian, you need a four-year degree, a dietetic internship, have to pass a grueling exam, and to compete with other job applicants, a master's degree is essential. In fact, effective 2024, a master's degree will be required. In addition, CapMed ranked foodservice supervisors over the dietitians. Making food, taking food preferences, and any and all glorified foodservice duties were piled upon us atop the clinical responsibilities.

"I was trying to explain to my friend, who's a nurse, there are four main areas of practice: clinical, food service, community, and management," said Veteran, that most senior of dietitians at CapMed. "She was wondering where all I could work if I wanted to leave this messed-up place. Wellness could be its own thing, too, I guess. Anyway, I told her that management typically pays the most, and she asked me why I didn't do management here since I've been here so long, because she also knows all my gripes about this place and how it definitely needs changing here. So, I just told her they pick who they want. It's who you know or something. Definitely not what you know."

"You know what I hate," added Tanya, a dietitian who worked outside the facility most of the time, "Ever-body thinks they're a 'nutritionist.' Sure, some people might be, but GET A LICENSE. Ever-one can play "Wonderwall" too, but that don't make 'em guitarists, and slappin' a

Band-aid on a cut don't mean you're a surgeon now. C'mon, girls!"

It irks most registered, licensed dietitians when "nutritionists" are on TV promoting diets and nutritional supplements that really aren't clinically proven or possibly safe.

"And don't get me started on Dr. Oz! Did you know that most physicians only have ONE nutrition class? JUST ONE. They are not the experts on this, people!" Tanya continued her rant.

"Right?" said Jessica, "And finally, if you are a family member, please don't ask me for meal plans or weight loss advice at the family reunion. Cousin Dirk, I'm not out here asking you for free welding services, not asking Hattie for free haircuts just because she's in beauty school!"

Chapter 13: Animal Magnetism

In early June, I was sunning in a fold-out lawn chair in my yard. The garden was tilled with the help of my "renter," Brad Pit (again, not joking, that's his name), and it was now time to relax and tan. Unfortunately, the weekends were becoming more precious as my work environment was less of a happy place. I tried telling my mom some of the issues with Miss Sweets, but there were only two responses she ever gave, so I finally just sucked it up and moved forward with my life:

Response one: "Well, quit, then."

Response two: "There ain't no perfect job, Jolene."

Mom was a realist.

No sooner did I have my Crisco on (I was out of tanning oil, and I already told you how far it was to get to town) and my bikini arranged right when I felt the Gift of Sight descend upon me. My eyes opened, and immediately a small phoebe lit upon my bare midriff. Reaching out and cupping the bird in my hands, I waited for a message that never came. Five seconds passed, and the little bird flew away.

This wasn't the first communion I'd had with an animal. There'd been good and bad interactions, but way more than most humans will have in a lifetime. Based upon these encounters, I'd discerned some animals (birds, deer, cats, for example) are kindred spirits with me while others (snakes, *MEAN* dogs—not good boys, bear) are set against me in this life. I've tried to find some Biblical reason why these animals, in particular, take sides as they do, but there is no logic.

Snakes, of course, since Genesis (Chapter 3, I think), were cursed after Satan used that form to trick the humans into a deadly betrayal. Dogs ate the body of an evil lady named Jezebel in II Kings, and bears mauled 42 kids in II Kings, too. II Kings is a brutal chapter. But ravens would peck your eyes out in Proverbs 30:17. So my Biblical Sight and Gift of animal affinity (Don't call it "Familiar" -- too witch-crafty) definitely didn't fall within any obvious guidelines.

There was no handbook for the weird way I was made. I'd learned long ago to keep my mouth shut about what was going on inside my mind. Familiar with the DSM-4 (1994 Diagnostic and Statistical Manual of Mental Disorders), voices, visions, and Snow-White level animal encounters confessed to a counselor were only going to result in a 48-hour hold and psychiatric medication. After working in a behavioral health facility out west, I also knew there was often a religious component to psychosis. Telling was not an option.

When I had first returned to the area, I'd tried to get back into bow-hunting as a stress-relieving therapy. Often, I would just sit in the woods, no pressure to shoot anything, one with nature. An entire season would pass, deer five feet from camouflaged, scent-free me as I simply enjoyed the proximity. Then, winter and snowfall would descend, and I would bundle up and head deep into the oak trees, barren of leaves, and nestle into a hollow trunk. On more than one occasion, a yearling would look directly at my form, swiveling its brown-and-white head, trying to decipher the puzzle of my identity. Then, the creature would cautiously move within inches before backing, then running, away because something, instinctually, tells them to fear this thing they've never even seen before—a human.

Human animals are so much harder to navigate than all others. According to the Bible teachings we learned growing up, everybody is born sinful. Everybody is selfish. We have to fight against it if we want to do right, but without the help of Jesus, we are hopeless because there is no way we can go head-to-head against Satan and his army of demons.

Before I became a nice-looking person, I only had to deal with my own issues. Once you're a woman and you become attractive to men, you have to deal with their issues, too. I'm not complaining. I believe that ugly people are the last frontier of permissible discrimination. Studies prove that attractive people are more often chosen and have more confidence, and as someone who has been on both sides of the coin, I can attest this is true.

The "Me Too! Movement" has considerably helped expose much of what women endure, so my hopes are high that my daughter will inherit a changed society. Of course, Our Lady was a safe working environment before the Movement. Still, I'd had difficult experiences prior: that manager at the Mexican restaurant who got me in a headlock, that preacher who tried to kiss me in the food pantry.

I wasn't even giving off any signals to those psychos, quite the opposite. When the restaurant manager finally released me, he strangely, calmly said:

"You think you're so young and tough, don't you?" This was 30 years ago. I thought he would murder me and drag me into the walk-in cooler because I've always watched a lot of true-crime programs like *Dateline* and *48 Hours*.

The preacher (Not my church preacher, mom, don't go murder him) was just another volunteer at a food pantry, and immediately after the random attack, which I rebuffed, became panicked and apologetically cried:

"You've just got to understand, my wife and I sleep in separate beds!" And he wouldn't be the last man during my lifetime to pull a similar stunt and use the separate beds plea.

I could recall almost ten egregious incidents and hundreds of innocent inquiries. A man actually wrecked his car while cat-calling me and ran right into a light post—instant Karma.

But looks don't guarantee marital success, and looks can also decrease the likelihood that other women will want to be your friend, and my being religious and strange and now out of sync with the church by way of divorce didn't help matters. But, interestingly enough, the older I got, the less powerful my looks became, and the more likely girls and women befriended me. It seemed that my flaws made me more desirable to them.

Chapter 14: Hope Springs Temporarily

As calendars turned to July 2020, I became the most efficient version of myself. Jessica was beginning to reveal small details of her life to me. If she needed to leave early, I would offer to take her remaining patients. When she seemed upset one morning, I gave her space but told her I was available to help with her work or just to talk. Respect was being gained, and a relationship was being established.

Jessica's best friend, Kate, was an easy-going hippy-chick and likely catalyst to the betterment of my relationship with Jessica. She would come into our freezing workspace, the scent of formaldehyde wafting through the vents, and regale us with stories of her past life as a roadie/backup drummer for a local band. She claimed to have a shrine to Chris Cornell in her home and would later take a vacation day every year on the anniversary of his death. We bonded over our shared love of music, and she would be the only person at work who would ever know the details of my early life as a child banjo prodigy.

When at least two or more dietitians, therapists, or other staffers gathered in the office, conversations were now happening freely in my presence, without whispering or exchanged looks between the others. I was becoming a trusted member of the group. My side had been chosen.

I was also starting to see familiar faces, refugees of the Loveless shut-down. The state of Kentucky had tried to intervene on behalf of the local community near the old Our Lady building, citing a need for COVID overflow rooms. Still, Loveless had moved on, and further negotiation was closed. Then, in a matter of months,

MegaDocs had swooped in, buying up buildings at pennies on the dollar, but never re-opening the hospital again.

Finally, the decision was made to go above Sweets and talk to Prudence about Miss Sweets' lack of response where I was concerned. She listened intently, took notes, even. Then, the following week, her announcement:

"I've decided to retire. COVID is just too much for me. My final day is the 10th." My words had been wasted.

Chapter 15: Outta Here

"I hate this place!!" screamed one of the kitchen crew members as she stormed out the swinging doors, tore off her hairnet, flashed the supervisor a select appendage, and followed with "I QUIT!" For once, I'd had time to take my 15-minute break, so I saw the whole thing go down and hastily reported back to the office to share.

"I want to quit, too, but I need money," lamented Jessica. Daisy sat in shock, disbelieving anyone would be so daring. Kate had come by to hear the exciting tale. For a brief moment, we could all live vicariously through this bold woman.

Kate spoke up, deciding she might have a solution to Jessica's problem: "Ok, Jessica, if you really need money bad, you could always be a mistress. You heard about Bill Gates, didn't you? Well, now it's out that he has these *naked* pool parties. I can tell by that squint in your eyes that you have a disgusted face under your mask, but just hear me out! The question of the day is: what's worse, working here or just going to a naked pool party with some rich ugly guy about once a month?"

"Daisy, close your ears!" Jessica squawked. "Woohoo, that's hilarious."

"At this point, I'm gonna have to go with Bill Gates," I said, "because that giant dog tried to tip over my car again this morning, and I just don't feel safe driving here anymore!" I had told them all before about my battles with Cujo, which continued after my first week of so-called "training" with Miss Sweets.

I also tended to see lots of wildlife on my way in, but thus far had effectively dodged it all, minus one unfortunate squirrel.

Jessica always found friendly stray cats and sometimes farm animals in unexpected locations during her commute, but occasionally even at work. She had walked between buildings just a week before, finding three abandoned kittens, which she lovingly fostered. On her way home that same night, she'd seen a rooster standing in the middle of the highway near the XXX joints and gambling hotspots. You can imagine the jokes we told and would continue to tell.

Daisy always had pet stories about horses, rabbits, and the occasional coonhound. Her stories tended to involve a lot of human characters as well. She liked to speculate on the human-animal interactions that likely created bad animal behavior. Nurture versus nature.

Typically, Kate had no animal stories because she lived in the city and claimed to see no animals at all. I don't think she believed half of what we told her. All the other girls that came and went through the office primarily had domesticated animals as pets. When they heard the story about Cujo, they didn't ask about me or my car. Instead, they said, "Is Cujo alright?", and that is the true sign of a city person or a person who a canine has never terrorized on a dark country road. Or maybe they'd never read any Stephen King and therefore didn't understand the viciousness of a dog called "Cujo."

After the other girls had gone about their days and only three of us remained, the conversation shifted to the Nutrition Director position that Prudence had left wide open.

"This is why you were brought here! You could be the one to make CapMed a better place," Jessica and Kate said, pumping me up and encouraging me to apply. "There is no way Sweets can make it through an interview without telling lies, and Georgia's face will turn red, and she'll get mad about something."

63

I was listening but not yet convinced. I was still so new to this place, and my job was easy other than being underappreciated, hated, and tormented by the occasional mental warfare. Skills were downplayed, needs were left unmet. Management required delicate handling of interpersonal relations, so many of which this place had botched over the years that a team of therapists would need calling in to fix. Then there was the matter of Sweets. The Nutrition Director was probably going to need to get her in line. Was I capable of running this department? Yes. Was I a better choice than Sweets and Georgia? Oh, yes. Did the other employees need a fair and balanced leader? Yes. But was this what I wanted for me? I still didn't know.

The day Prudence left, she caught me in the hallway and pulled me aside. "I know that Sweets is the weakest link here, and I pity whoever takes my job because they will be doing hers, too. I shouldn't tell you all this, but they will never fire her. So nothing is going to change here. Good luck." And with that, she was gone.

I'm not sure if Prudence was commiserating with me, giving me a warning, apologizing for her inactivity, or all three. Regardless of the reason, I decided to proactively start documenting all my interactions with Sweets, in case of Sweets' falsely accused me as she had other dietitians in the past. My senses told me a storm was brewing, and I would need to be above reproach. So, I secretly went to the Director of Human Resources, Donna, and wrote out all my concerns about the hostility and bullying, including the long, unpaid work hours which I knew were illegal; I'd been a manager, myself, after all! Unfortunately, Donna had to leave for a meeting, but she seemed concerned and asked me to leave a copy of the complaint on her desk, which I did.

Chapter 16: Asparagus Pee

"You all, I'm getting fat as a little pig, and I don't even care," exclaimed Tanya. "My husband told me, 'you best get control of that, woman,' but guess what? I don't care because he ain't even in control of hisself! I could change if I wanted to, but I don't," she declared.

"You go, girl," Veteran encouraged. "Meanwhile, I'm over here struggling and look, I'm a dietitian, so I know what should work. I hate it when I get clients wanting weight loss information because it's like, here's your answer: eat less and exercise more."

"Depression works well for me. The pounds just roll right off," mumbled Jessica. "I know that 'eat less and exercise more' is the answer for most people, but some people have serious metabolic problems, so it won't work. As for me, exercising more means less sleep, which means I can't deal with stress, so is that really a solution? Too complicated. This is why I work inpatient. Sick people ain't worried about their looks. *Usually.*"

"I once went on a fad diet and lost 13 pounds in like six weeks, and I wasn't even overweight when I started. It was the "Raw" diet, so mostly organic uncooked fruits and vegetables. The meat was supposed to be raw, too, but I fudged that part and just mostly ate nuts, instead," I said. "I felt like I was nineteen years old again. Felt amazing."

"So, you were a vegan," said Jessica flatly.

"NO, nothing was cooked, and I did eat some meat, like maybe three meals a week, but I cooked it because I was scared. Oh, and I also ate Junior Mints. I had a weird craving for them at that time."

"Honey, California made you so weird," commented Tanya. "But if you felt so good, then why did you stop?"

I told them all the truth: "That whole spinach/E.coli thing happened, and I realized humans were pooping on all of them raw vegetables, so I went out that very day and got me a donut."

Everybody roared. When the laughter subsided, Veteran asked a follow-up question that transitioned into the week's major discussion, asparagus pee.

"You still paying a bunch extra for any organic food?"

"Only milk," I answered, "and just because it tastes better."

"Yeah, me, too," she agreed. "Which brand do you buy?"

I told her, then she asked me: "You notice anything 'fishy' about it?"

Veteran's story: Veteran ate salmon once a week on Friday night (she wasn't Catholic but knew she needed more healthy fats, so she just scheduled this to get it over with. She hated fish.) This was a Tuesday afternoon, and she noticed a strong fishy smell when she went to pee. *Oh, lord, is there something wrong down there?* She thought to herself. She hadn't eaten fish in days, but it didn't make any sense either way. She was busy and forgot about it all until the next day around the same time in the afternoon when the same thing occurred. *Something is going on!*

Being a dietitian, she decided to review everything she had consumed over the past 24 hours. Nothing was out of the ordinary, but when she was preparing her breakfast cereal the following day, she noticed that her milk was fortified with Omega-3 fatty acids. She turned to the nutrition facts label, and there it was! Those healthy fats were sourced from fish. She had been drinking fish milk.

When the story ended, there was a mixture of disgust (From Daisy), intrigue (from Erin, the remote dietitian), happiness (from me, because I, too, thought something was wrong 'down there'), and newfound interest in the purchase of fish milk from the rest.

"This brings up an interesting point," Kate commented. "You know how supposedly some people either can or cannot smell asparagus in pee or something like that? I wonder if this is the same? Are there some people who cannot smell the fish pee?"

There was a smattering of laughter, followed up by Erin's account of being an intern at a state university where asparagus pee was studied. First, all the interns ate asparagus, then peed at intervals into marked cups, like at the doctor's office. Then, the interns had to smell the different urines—everybody's urine.

The outcome? Erin couldn't remember.

"Listen, I'll smell asparagus- and fish-pee all day if I never have to smell what I smelled yesterday again," said Veteran.

"Oh no, you all. I'm a-leavin' if you all are gonna do this agin," lamented Daisy.

"You better get on out the door, then," commanded Vet, and with that, Daisy gathered up her things and was gone.

"The Worst Thing I've Ever Smelled" was not a game, so much as a comparison. Vomit due to a GI bleed. C-Diff diarrhea. Burning hair. Infected foot wounds. Gas being expelled from a colostomy bag. It was like that song "My Favorite Things" from *The Sound of Music,* except in reverse. There was never a consensus on a winner. They were all agreeably terrible.

"There are plenty of people smart enough to work in hospitals, but some people just don't have the stomach for it," Kate observed.

I thought back to a kid in middle school, dry heaving when somebody else threw up on the school bus. Anytime I smelled sawdust, I thought of that kid.

Chapter 17: Power Struggles

August 2020

"$400.00? Okay, let me grab my card." The previous couple of weeks had been enough to stir me to action. Working with a professional resumé builder and interview coach was my new hobby as I planned for workplace domination. Unfortunately, the manager-employee relationship between Sweets and me had devolved into a middle-school level argument, complete with gossip girls and cold-shouldered stare-downs. Sweets had to be stopped.

She rarely looked at or spoke to me anymore, but one morning in the hallway, she brightly quipped, "It's too bad you can't apply for the Director's job. You know that when we hired you here, Prudence knew she would be leaving. So, she knew if she hired you that you would be blocked from getting that job."

At the time, I was taken aback and quickly countered, "I don't want that job, anyway, Miss Sweets," then walked off. And that was true at the time, I didn't really want that job. But I was beginning to feel that it was my duty as a qualified candidate to take it. Sweets was trying to get in my head.

She had enlisted Georgia in her war against me, trying to expose a crack in my polished work exterior. Each night, Georgia would remove all the paper from the industrial-sized six-tray printer so I would have to restart, refill, and wait when I ran morning reports. Sabotaging the work environment by unplugging computers and revoking access to applications was another favorite tactic.

Georgia's primary modus operandi was a form of a human house of cards, basically piling more and more tasks upon a foundation of one small person (me), gleefully awaiting the collapse of the whole. If I needed to leave "on time" at day's end for once to pick up my daughter, I had to report to Sweets before lunch, but preferably 48-hours ahead of time. Georgia would coincidentally appear on the day of the needed timely exit, demanding a last-minute task be completed.

There were drawbacks to having the Sight. I couldn't always control when It came to me or where It took me. I couldn't "See" where blood relatives were concerned; It had never been a great parenting tool. The old adage "Ignorance is bliss" comes to mind.

As Sweets and Georgia colluded to discredit me, I was faced with knowing that I worked for completely dishonest people. Every scandalous thing I had been hearing about them was true. I could See the evidence.

In the sanctuary of her office, Georgia had jotted down lies on a steno pad: late every day, rude to patients, bossy to staff, acts like better than others (Okay, maybe I was guilty of that one sometimes), doesn't do work, mean to kitchen staff. At the top of the pad? One name: Jolene. So, when they were piling more and more work on me, I was determined to do it all to spite them.

Good things came from the Sight, too, like one summer when my ex-husband was mowing the lawn, and I pulled in the driveway, stepped out of my car, and immediately threw my body to the ground. A rock got sucked up and zipped out of that mower and shattered the car window where I had been standing. Brain damage or death, averted! Of course, I knew only a second before it happened. But in the case of the current workplace drama,

I knew plenty of time in advance. At least I could prepare an offensive strategy.

Chapter 18: A Gift or A Curse

There was no magic school owl with an invitation, no prideful, passed-down lineage. This was something not talked about. You needed to hide this just like people used to hide mental illness before it was better understood. The ramifications of exposing the Sight could be anywhere from ex-communication to incarceration. What if I knew the details of a crime? Any jury would convict me.

I'd learned that It had to be used very precisely, like a surgeon's scalpel, if I actively pursued the use of It at all. As I've previously said, It came to me uninvited, also. There were consequences. Lies sometimes needed to be told, like when I confronted my ex-husband. To cover my explanations of how I knew things, I'd bluff, practicing my poker face beforehand for hours.

The lies could potentially impact innocent bystanders. For instance, if I were to confront Sweets, would I tell her that Georgia told me everything they were plotting against me? How else would I know?

Other worries reigned in my momentum as I prepared to battle for my good name. Were the things I Saw really real this time, just because they had been in the past? Taking heed of some Biblical advice to be slow to get angry about things (It's all over Proverbs and Ephesians), I tried to block my mind from the internal conversations that sometimes played on loop. I worried that maybe even if the things I Saw were real, I could still have schizophrenia and not a Gift. Although It had been helpful to open my eyes to harsh realities, I could see how access to too much of the private machinations of my nemesis could've led me down a dark path. I didn't want to fall into that madness again.

One morning while relaxing in a warm bath, head back, eyes closed, something caused me to sit up abruptly, water sloshing forward, then back in a singular wave. As always, I had scanned the enclosure for spiders or any sign of life before submerging myself. Yet the wing-like flutter, sometimes mimicked by the rubbing together of fingers, blasted in my left ear, and despite frantically scanning, there was no sign of the insects that for once I hoped would be the cause, only a blank white wall. My heart pounded, and I prayed to God to be near me. The episodes were coming closer together, and I was scared.

Chapter 19: The Other Side

We continued to have at least weekly impromptu talks in the dietitian's office, Jessica and Daisy, and sometimes Kate or the other dietitians and therapists in attendance. These typically included a highlight reel of sorts, with everybody blurting out the best, usually funniest but not always, happenings from the week.

"We saw some freakish creature on Saturday on our way to the Amish donut shop, and now I'm completely obsessed with it, and I want to show you guys." I excitedly pulled up a picture of a silver fox, a particular one like my daughter and I saw, all black and gray with red-orange eyes.

"Is that a coyote?" asked Daisy.

"No, it's called a silver fox, and it's rare around these parts. The funny thing is, my daughter remembered one from a TV show, but when she typed 'silver fox' into the search engine, all these good-looking old men came up instead," I said.

"Huh?" asked Daisy, but I didn't explain that part.

I was a fast talker and, moving right along with my story, went on: "That fox, it looked me right in the eyes. It was standing on the edge of a cornfield right beside the road at the end of the day. It was still light out. The eyes were speaking to me, telling me I was going to die. I looked up fox symbolism later that night, and it can mean all kinds of things, but it can be a bad omen."

"Are you sure it didn't say 'you are going to diet,'" joked Kate, knowing I wasn't being 100% serious about my impending death.

"We all have to die sometime, though. Hebrews 9:27 says, 'it is appointed unto men to die. Maybe you'll be 90 years old. Nobody can know it," advised Daisy.

"So now we're all dying. Thanks a lot, Daisy," Jessica said.

Daisy asked, "Anyways, did you guys hear about that nurse up near Morgantown who killed all those patients?"

"I heard about that on the news last night," I answered, "and I was wondering if she didn't have something bad wrong with her, like an untreated mental illness."

"It freaks me out when psychotic people think they see demons," Jessica replied, possibly commenting on a different story than the one we'd been discussing. "I mean, like, think about that guy in the Bible that had demons cast out of him, and then the demons went into those pigs, and the pigs went crazy and drowned."

I was quiet, no comment.

Daisy took the opportunity to disrupt everyone's comfort by quoting Ephesians 6:12, reminding us all that evil, unseen forces are all around us, all the time. Literally, demons were just standing right beside you.

"What if, then, some people—now, I'm not saying everyone is going to fit into this group—but some people who are diagnosed with schizophrenia are actually being tormented by demons, and they are the only ones who can see them? Maybe these people are destined for greatness, so Satan uses these demons to hurt them and to decrease their credibility with other humans because other humans never would believe this mumbo-jumbo?" After I said all this, everyone just sat silently for a few beats.

"I don't want to think about that," answered Jessica.

Chapter 20: Fall and Falling

"These dang ladybugs," hollered Mom as she stood barefoot on her porch with the Shop-Vac, hose sucking up insects in droves.

Known locally as ladybugs, the look-alikes were Asian beetles brought in by the government to feed wild turkeys. That was the rumor, anyway. Evidently, the experiment went wrong, and the bugs took over. They became a plague, descending on the community each fall in hoards, clacking against windshields like hailstones, embedding into porch floorboards and behind shutters. They would leave a tarry sienna trail along any surface or wall they chose to travel, a winding line that was hard to clean, even with bleach. Asian beetles were hatching out three months early that year, probably due to global warming.

There were "stinkbugs," too, that we knew weren't the stinkbugs of our youth. They were just something similar that hatched in the spring and sounded like a helicopter in flight. These stinkbugs were ugly but harmless, and we had come to accept them as a necessary evil of country life. The ladybugs were the stinky bunch. Mom and I bought and used every legal or home-brewed chemical we could afford to combat those smelly varmints, but they just kept coming, like the spider in the king's palace (Proverbs 30:28.) There was no stopping them.

"It's the end times," prophesied Mom. "You see the news? They's fires all over out there where you lived." The truth was, there had always been fires in California. It was nothing new, but I didn't want to argue that day.

"That's terrible," I answered. "I hope people are making it to safety. But before the world ends, I brought you that spray I picked up over in Steeltown after work yesterday. Also, I'm applying for the big job at work, so I wondered if I could use your printer?"

"Well, that ain't gonna make old Skeletor your friend, honey. What if you don't get it? She's a-gonna know you tried to get above her," Mom warned.

Confidently I replied, "I'm the most qualified, I've got the most experience out of all of us, and nobody else is going to want to come here!"

"Just stay humble now. Remember Proverbs 16:18, prides goes before a fall!" she countered.

"Mom, there's a difference between conceit and confidence. I'm just saying that these other two ladies are not qualified for the job, and that's me being nice about it. If I told you all the truth about them, you'd never believe it, anyway," I pouted.

"Now, honey, just listen to me for a minute," Mom soothed. "They's something off about that Sweet lady, I can feel it. The other one, she's probably just plain dumb. But the Sweet one ain't sweet at all, and you need to be careful around a person like that."

Chapter 21: Work Worries

Every week at least once a week, we tried to tune in to either West Virginia's "Big Jim" Jim Justice, who would appear with his English Bulldog, Baby Dog, or Ohio's Mike DeWine, who had the world's most animated sign language interpreter, to hear details and information about COVID-19. Unfortunately, we were less enchanted with Kentucky Governor Andy Beshear.

"He just repeats what DeWine says. It's like he watches Ohio and then does exactly that. And I can say that. I'm from Kentucky. You can't say that, Daisy," quipped Tanya.

As I've said before, Tanya was rarely in the office, tending to work remotely, falling into the category of department employee once terrorized and now ignored. Her past difficulties had included being accused of stealing the company car she had been assigned and being denied time off to attend her cousin's funeral, along with struggling to breathe in a fume of passive aggression for over six months. But she had made it through, and now she just made herself scarce. There was a glimmer of hope for change since Prudence had retired and left an open position, so she had been showing up more frequently, taking part in office chats.

Jessica, Kate, and two other dietitians were ranting about how we had to buy our own masks. "And I would like to know if Sweets and Georgia are buying masks? Somebody said they saw a box of masks in Georgia's office, and they look exactly like the brand the nurses have upstairs. Coincidence? I think not. But if they are getting masks, I bet Butt-Kisser #1 (an unnamed, lazy crony who lunched daily with Sweets) is getting in on them."

"Girls, speaking of butts, guess what happened to me?" Tanya recounted her most recent mishap in the home visit world. "This dirty old man grabbed my booty, and I told him, 'No, now, we don't do that', but he just kept on and was talking all kinds of nasty stuff. So, girls, I just said to myself, 'I don't have to put up with this.' I was so flustered, and I drove down to the Dairy Queen and was just goin' to pull in there, calm down, and maybe get me a Blizzard. So, I'm sitting there, and I see something in my peripheral vision, and honey, I look over, and two grown women are fighting! I mean, they're pullin' hair, they're punchin' each other, they end up down on the ground rollin' around. I mean, I just don't know, girls. I just don't know!"

At that point, I was both revolted and amused, but laughter came freely and uncontrollably for us all, as it would over the coming months as all the cringe-worthy events that happened to me and the others were recounted. The laughter subsided, then bubbled back up. Finally, an eerie silence settled over the room when Tanya looked up, face set hard: "I'm sure you all heard what that doctor up at Beckley did to his patients."

That afternoon, I'd found the Beckley story online, my stomach souring as I read how this man had molested his patients. Scrolling quickly past additional details, I glimpsed a frowning yet familiar face holding a numbered placard—the mugshot of a graying doctor who was sadly recognizable to me. Everything was so wrong, yet we were all victims of this terrible, inescapable machine.

Chapter 22: Common Ground

"Okay, you're at Bill Gates' pool party...." This is how our daily talks started out again and again now. It was a hilarious version of "would you rather" where somebody threw out random names, and you chose the least heinous suitor.

"Kim Jong-un or Mitch McConnell?" My query was met with a collective groan. Periodically, I sat at home on a weekend when a truly genius pair came to mind, and I sent a random text out to Jessica, laughing out loud at the absurdity.

Although each of us agreed we would never personally go through with such a thing in real life for any amount of money, it was fun to believe that for some women, there was a path to income that existed yet did not involve working 9 to 5 Monday through Friday. We demeaned ourselves in some ways, and those women demeaned themselves in some ways.

"Even though I could not and would not do it, I understand why some young girls end up doing what they do and I ain't gonna judge them," said Erin. Erin was the renal dietitian, worked remotely, and was rarely seen by other employees. She steered clear of the place to avoid any conflicts with management but had stopped by on this occasion to complete some required training on a yawn-inducing topic like thickened liquids.

"But won't those girls have regrets later in life," asked Daisy, "when they realize they've given something so precious to someone who really didn't care, and all just for money?"

"Wow," I said, no longer laughing, "that feels exactly like my time here."

"On an unrelated topic, I hate it when you spend thirty minutes sitting with a patient, whatever, then the next day you go in, and there is a bedbug sign or a lice sign or even a COVID sign on the door!" Jessica lamented. We all began griping about this long-standing communication problem, now complicated and life-threatening due to COVID-19.

"Well, when they find out someone is positive for COVID, it would be nice to tell me, since I don't get a respirator mask or nothin' and I'm just in there, breathin' up the germs," stated Tanya.

"Good luck with that," Jessica countered, "because you might remember when I had the nerve to ask for regular surgical masks." I knew the story. Jessica had been the victim of "Hurricane Georgia," a flurry of masks and face shields flung upon her due to her audacity.

"Something's got to be done, people," said Tanya, "these managers ain't right! Daisy saw a whole box of masks in Miss Sweets' office, but they won't give any to us, and *they* don't even go see patients!"

"I've sent in my application for the Director job, so we'll see what happens," I said.

"Oh, lord, this place is more corrupt than a prison! We gotta pray that something comes of it." Even the veteran, with her tactic of isolation as self-preservation, was coming around to hoping for change.

Chapter 23: Sorry, Not Sorry

September 2020

"You can't apply for this job, sorry." Human Resources representative "Alexandria" was a sledgehammer in human form, blunt and heavy. "You don't have enough experience here to move up."

Perplexed, I countered, "I have *decades* of experience. I only took this non-management job because it was the only one open, but now this job has come open, and I'd like to apply."

"I'm sorry, but it doesn't work that way here. All that matters is what you've done here, so nothing you did before matters anymore. It looks like you're entry-level. Sorry."

I left the meeting in a state of shock, which was becoming a common occurrence at CapMed. The day passed, and I fact-checked with the HR Director, Donna, knowing this must be misinformation, but the responses did not vary.

"What madness is this???" Jessica screeched as we discussed this news in our cubicles. "Just one more way to block anybody qualified from getting ahead!"

Personally, I was reeling and also coming to terms with the fact that I would not be recouping the money I had invested into a now unusable resumé and hours of hopeful interview coaching. When Mom found out, I would have to eat crow, and if her predictions came to pass, Sweets and Georgia would be out for blood.

That week, two things happened in privacy and secrecy, and even I didn't *See* them.

The first thing that happened was that a document was forged.

Jessica felt powerful and led the secret charge to open up the Nutrition Director interviews to any candidates. Amidst hushed whispers, signatures were gathered, a document was crafted, and alliances forged. There were only a select group of invitees. Being a brown-noser guaranteed exclusion from the secret mission of letting the President of CapMed know what was happening. There was a viable candidate within the ranks being railroaded! There were incompetent ninnies already in power! An investigation was warranted! The alarm was sounded to the highest level and not anonymously.

Jessica scanned the document into her work e-mail and pressed "send." After that, there was no going back. The group's opinion was that The President would probably be stunned to learn that these things were happening and respond immediately to such allegations.

The second thing that happened was a private hiring session. Behind the closed door of Prudence's past domain, Sweets and Georgia perched atop rigid office chairs, awaiting the one and only candidate they intended to interview. Jonas showed up 30 minutes early, wearing an "I Love the Lord" face mask and full suit-tie combo.

"Oh, it's just so good to see y'all again! I'm just so blessed to have the opportunity!"

This was the same young grad that Georgia had wanted to hire instead of me a couple of months prior when Jessica had put her foot down and demanded an experienced candidate. The current dietitian job up for grabs was only part-time, but it was still traditional to advertise and interview multiple candidates.

Jonas still wasn't qualified for the position, but Sweets and Georgia were using a loophole to get him hired. They wanted someone who knew less than they did and someone who would owe them gratitude and servitude in return for a job not deserved. A deal was struck. Promises were made. Only Sweets and Georgia failed to tell Jonas to keep their secrets.

Chapter 24: Monthly Meeting

Miss Sweets was sitting out in the open area of the office. Daisy, Kate, Tanya, and the gang gathered in for the monthly meeting, only halfway social distancing, in the cheap Chinese surgical masks they'd ordered online. Jessica stayed in her cubicle, angrily typing, refusing to respect the host. Sweets' mask was hovering down over her black-mustached upper lip, falling into her mouth as she spoke and finally surrendering to her chin. Thank heaven for cooler weather because closed-toe shoes were finally forced upon those neglected feet.

Following subjection to a protracted description of her sister's daughter's gallbladder surgery, I was struggling with a rising fury over this woman's incompetence. She continued to drone on for a total of about twenty minutes, during which, despite the mask, I must have exhibited a look of sheer boredom. Sweets locked eyes with me.

"Moving along," she sneered, "I need to let you all know that there are about to be some big changes around here. Jobs are going to be looked at. If people don't start doing more work, they could be in trouble. Some hospitals would fire people who don't do the work they are asked to do. As a matter of fact,-we are looking into that right now."

A brief silence was broken by Kate: "What standard are we supposed to be meeting, exactly?"

Sweets replied, "That will be told to you later, once it's all figured out. Meanwhile, we have interviewed for the part-time job and have chosen someone. I'm sure everyone will like him."

I couldn't take it anymore. "Wait, why are you hiring someone if you are looking at eliminating a position? I was the last one hired on, so if a position would be eliminated, it would be mine. I would rather have part-time hours than no hours, so I will do that new position if it comes to that. If you just tell me exactly what it is you want me to do, I will meet the standard, but at this point, all I know to do is what the Big Green Bible tells me."

Yes! I had finally put it all out there. Finally, everyone was present and had witnessed the exchange, and Sweets had been called out on her failed passive-aggressive technique. She was messing up, threatening to fire someone yet hiring someone new. She was invalidating her own arguments.

But my personal drama got lost in the collective cry: "You hired someone, and not a one of us sat in on interviews??"

Sweets responded and said, "We can hire anyone we want, and you don't have to be included." Double Yes! Sweets was going to lose all her powers of persuasion with this group.

"Okay, but why did we already hire someone when that clinic isn't even built yet?" Erin inquired in the most respectful tone possible.

"Non-managers wouldn't understand, but there is a lot of work and planning that has to happen even before that," stated Sweets, firmly signaling the end of the discussion.

Chapter 25: Hindsight

Before the day got into full swing one September morning, the daily talk started out with Daisy telling us about her daughter's new job working as an assistant at a veterinary clinic. "I always wanted to be a veterinarian when I was growing up. Later I just realized I wasn't smart enough. But I did get to be a mom, and I always wanted to do that, too, and to own horses."

"You are VERY smart, Daisy. That just wasn't the Lord's plan for you," I remarked.

Jessica interjected, "Well, if it makes you feel any better, there are a bunch of people here in big jobs who are dumber than all of us put together."

Everybody laughed, and I said, "Well, honestly, every hospital I've worked in has at least one doctor that none of the employees would ever even let operate on a stray dog. Seriously, it's an open secret that if your co-worker comes through the ER and *that* doctor is the one on-call, then you better pray for a miracle."

"Well, I just wish I would've been a dietitian like you two," lamented Daisy.

"The grass must always be greener on the other side! Jessica and I just had this discussion two days ago about how we should've been nurses. We would be making more money and have our school paid for, but here we are making less money and owing student loans," I griped.

"Right? And nurses get to work longer shifts over fewer days, so they come here less days. They can actually get other stuff done during the week, so they don't have to use up all their time off! As a bonus, they use up less gas money, too, and gas costs like $10.00 a gallon now! But, still, I wouldn't want to wipe butts," said Jessica. "For all the time we've put in, we should've just gone to med school."

Going into a nursing program was discouraged when I was in college due to "oversaturation." However, dietetics was a new and expanding field with promise of flexibility and untold riches. I chuckled as I remembered the bright vision of my future. I spent the summer of 1991 driving thirteen hours in my Honda Civic to a summer job in the Catskills. A "nutritionist" at a weight loss camp that no longer exists, I cheerfully designed menus, led aerobics classes, and educated teenagers on healthy eating— making a difference in the health of individuals—making an impact on the health of our nation. More recently, I had become the embodiment of every Gen-X female cliché: fifty, dissatisfied, no known retirement, and starting over in a hated job. My daughter said I reminded her of the cat lady on her *BoJack Horseman* cartoon, but I didn't know what that meant. She just said the cat had a lot of regrets.

Chapter 26: Piano Hands

"I'm just sayin', how do people get so far in these deals that they do crazy stuff like kill their own kids and all?" observed Kate. She was wondering aloud why people like Lori Vallow and Chad Daybell may have killed Lori's children sometime in the past months. The general consensus was that it was possibly related to extreme Doomsday religious beliefs. I admit this line of conversation was my fault, prompted by my tales of Mom's "end times" fears.

"Hey, who knows?" I interjected, "Not murder, but I did have a preacher tell me God was going to cut my hands off once."

Five people were staring at me, stunned.

"Well, you just can't say something like that and not explain it!" exclaimed Veteran.

Jessica added, "Yeah, like, what kind of cult did you grow up in, woman?"

"That ain't right," Daisy said.

Tanya just sat there, shaking her head.

"Look," I said, "I think there might be extremists in all religions. This guy, he got the youth pastor job at our church starting when I was about a sophomore in high school…." Then I told them the story of piano hands:

"I was once a pretty good banjo player, but suffice it to say, my hand got hurt in an accident, and then I wasn't anymore. So, my mom started taking me to piano lessons. The piano teacher was almost 100 years old and liked to brag that she had crossed the Ohio River in a horse-drawn buggy one time when it was frozen over. She was a no-nonsense type, but I hated the piano and never practiced. I wasn't terrible at it, but I wasn't Liberace or nothin'. I hated those lessons, but my mom wouldn't let me quit.

Once my mom let you start some instrument or sport, there was no going back ('Quitters never win!'). The only way I got out of them lessons was finally after about eight years my teacher died.

Long story short (not really), about this same time, we were one of the first families to get a satellite and MTV, and I watched it all the time—Duran Duran, Cyndi Lauper, all that—and also, I stopped going to Wednesday night church. The teenagers went to 'Youth Group,' not regular church on Wednesday nights. There was a lesson, some food, a game, all fine, but this guy we're talking about was the preacher, and so I didn't go. I didn't go because when I was in Middle School, when I was timid and awkward and all, he tried to force me to play piano in the church. There was no possible way I had the musical ability or confidence to play before a live audience, so I said, 'No,' which was also really hard for me at that age.

In response, he said, 'That's fine, but if you have the musical gift of piano and don't use it for The Lord, He will see fit to take your hands.'"

"OH, MY HEAVENS!!" Exclaimed Veteran, "Please tell me this man is no longer preaching or teaching the youth of America?!"

"Nope, he's dead," I answered but continued, in true Daisy-style. "So, all those years later, I'm sitting home on that Wednesday night enjoying my MTV, and there's a knock on the door. I got up and saw Bucky Mayer at the door, who was this goofy kid in the grade above mine, and then behind him, there's this preacher man. 'Can we come in?' he asked, and I was like, 'Okay.' Because you don't be rude to adults, even if they curse your hands and all. Anyway, to get to the point, they come around the sofa, and this man's eyes were giant, and the look on his face was like, 'Get thee behind me, Satan.' I turned around and realized I still got MTV on, and Van Halen's "Hot for Teacher" video is on there in all its glory, with some teacher stripper-dancing on a school desk, all gyrating and flipping her hair crazy all around!"

By this point, the others were doubled over with laughter, and I'd started laughing and couldn't talk anymore, although the story was essentially complete, other than Bucky saying, "I love this video."

Chapter 27: Trainwreck

October 2020

"You are supposed to be in harassment prevention training. Just wondering why you aren't down here?" The voice on the extension was coming from a conference room where various educational sessions were held.

"I had no idea I was supposed to be in this. I have patients to see," I pleaded, but the voice commanded me to attend the training.

Apparently, my manager had signed me up for this course over a month before. I tried to call Sweets, but she ignored my calls true to form. So finally, I marched directly over to her office and, door ajar, she was visible. Facebook was pulled up on her company computer screen. I asked her about the training.

"I told you weeks ago. It is not up to me to remind you," she retorted.

Of course, she lied about telling me, and we both knew that, but, livid as I was, I could not allow it to show. She must have known by then that I had tried to apply for Prudence's old job. I rushed to the training and left all my patient care undone. The training lasted TWO FULL DAYS, not just one, and I wasn't sure how I would ever get caught up with my patients, but I tried to focus on the present and learn what I needed to pass the exit exam (Must score 80 of 100!)

An exorbitant amount of time—one full day—was spent on how to "talk someone down" and how to use restraints, if needed. A variety of holds and self-defense moves were practiced to exhaustion. In the facility where

I worked on behavioral medicine before CapMed, I'd just locked myself in a safe room and called security as needed.

I was feeling empowered that evening when I swung by Moms. She and my daughter were at the kitchen table, reading the paper and doing homework, respectively.

"Hey, one of you'uns, stand up here and let me show you how to get away from bad guys," I bragged. Wouldn't you know, Mom stood right up there and grabbed me from behind, and I did the moves with my arms, tried to get them up and break free, but she still had me.

"Well, that ain't no count," she chuckled, "Some man'd drag you off." I tried one more hold and got out, but I think she let me win that time.

Day two of the training, a different speaker showed up because the original had to get COVID testing. Instead of learning physical defense, this day was about mental defense.

"Like the sticks and stones bein' the physical and words bein' the mental," explained the speaker, a middle-aged male best described as that guy who always refers to his high school football glory days. "And it ain't like it used to be. You just can't go around calling people faggot or gay or stuff. Nope, we don't tolerate that."

His delivery is pretty rough around the edges, I thought. He drove his point home by telling a story so vulgar I could barely recount it to my co-workers later when I needed to explain to them why I was so angry.

"I don't even want to repeat it! He was so inappropriate! It's so gross, but he said this thing happened to him, that a male patient propositioned him in the facility and 'he don't swing that way,' and he said he told the guy 'buddy, I'm exit only.'"

"OH MY GOSH, what the crap??" hissed Jessica, "Are you kidding me??"

"No, not kidding," I said, but that's not the worst part.

After Gipper made a wreck of the sexual orientation portion of the day, it was on to sexual advances, followed by the program capstone, personal accounts.

"Look, people, there ain't no reason to take this thing overboard. If we know each other and I'm rubbing your shoulders, and you're ok with it, we can do that. A lot of people now you can't even touch 'em on the arm. Don't take it too far, ladies. Somebody can say you look good, okay? They're just bein' nice. Ain't no reason to get up in arms about it. There's a difference."

By that point, I was a bundle of energy. I wanted to lash out at this man, educate him on his ignorance and tell him why he was part of the problem. Looking around the room, I registered at least two other concerned faces on women, but they must have needed these jobs, and they were keeping quiet, too. We all saved it for the anonymous post-session questions every place had, where you rated the speaker and provided input.

The personal accounts' grand finale arrived, during which participants were given an hour to prepare a brief five-minute story about something related to discrimination or harassment that had impacted them. Although I had a treasure trove to choose from, I knew exactly which story needed retelling now:

Why I'm a Cat Person

When I was 18 years old and a sophomore in college, I lived off-campus in a townhouse-style apartment in a small Ohio town. Every afternoon I had a break between classes, so I would go home, change clothes, and complete a 5-mile run in the safe, residential neighborhood.

This particular day, I clipped on my WalkMan, turned up my music, and set out on foot as usual, but I was walloped in the lower leg when I was about two miles from home. Hit from behind, the impact caused me to stumble and fall onto the asphalt road, embedding small cinders into my knees and scuffing my palms as I tried to catch myself. My headphones were pulled from my ears, and I suddenly heard a woman screaming from the periphery. People were coming out to look at what was happening.

A dog was attacking me. Its jaws were attached to my right calf, and there was blood on the ground. An old woman ran out of a house, carrying a broom or some similar object overhead, to repel the dog, who must've feared the object because he released me. The old woman seemed to know the dog. I just got up and limped off, spotting a clinic at the end of the block. People were just standing around, gawking.

Reaching the clinic, I hobbled inside, signed in. I remember it was desolate there, like everyone else on the planet had someplace to be. I used the phone to call my mom, who lived an hour away. I was placed in a surgical green tile room with a transparent-paper-lined exam table.

The doctor came in immediately and closed the door behind him. He had on a white coat and carried a clipboard with paperwork attached. He began asking me the questions I assumed were on the paperwork, and then bent down to clean and look at the wound.

"I don't think you'll need stitches," he said, followed with "Um, so, do you have a boyfriend?"

I managed a "Yes," then the doctor stood up, asked me if I'd ever been to a gynecologist, and proceeded to give me a breast exam. I sat, stock still, arms straight down at my sides, thighs pressed together, calf still dripping blood, understanding what he was doing was likely wrong but unable to speak. I was paralyzed by fear and some misguided mixture of not wanting to be troublesome, respecting someone in authority, and respecting my elders. As soon as the "breast exam" was finished, I panicked as his hand slid down my stomach, saying my mom would be there any minute, and she'd told me I better be waiting for her out front.

That was the turning point of my life. When I went from being mentally healthy and trusting to understanding how easily it can all be taken away.

Chapter 28: Don't Pay to Complain

"I can't believe there was nowhere to complain about the speakers and the programming!" I'm still upset about the ridiculous "training" and views and values being espoused by the presenters. "What kind of place am I working for, anyway?" I bemoaned. "I mean, I'm gonna tell you all a secret... I even went to the Human Resources Director *months ago* and filed a complaint about the management in this department and never even heard another word about it... so I went down there to talk to *her* again, and she acted like she didn't know who I was or what I was talking about. The funny thing was, she said something like, 'I can't possibly know everyone here. It's not a small hospital like the one you came from!'"

"WHAT?" exclaimed Jessica, then followed with, "you should've been a smart alec and said, 'I thought you didn't know who I was, so how do you know where I worked before??'"

"I thought about it," I said, laughing, "but she didn't even give me a chance to reply, just told me that HR didn't need to communicate the course of action taken, if any, to a complaining employee unless that employee had been physically harmed. So I told her I was still being harassed, and she gave me a number I could call if I wanted to say more about it, so I called that."

"Oh, boy. Remember that past employee we told you about, 'Annie?'" Jessica asked. "She was so paranoid by the time she left here. She still maintains that the number you call to complain just loops back to Donna's secretary."

"But why would she do that," asked Daisy?

"She gets her bonus based on lack of complaints, is what I think," said Veteran.

"Oh, honey, this is how it is here, let me tell you. It's like basting a turkey. Layer after layer, and it's finally just on there thick, and the turkey is cooked, honey, and you're the turkey, and you didn't even realize the oven was burning you up," Tanya always had a countrified way to commiserate. "That woman up there in Human Resources, she ain't worth a hoot!"

"That's true about HR. She's never helped any of the people from our department. As far as I can tell, she always takes management's side in the end. But back to that stupid class; do you know when I did that class that there were people who didn't even get to tell their stories because one man went and wrote a five-page manuscript about his time being 'falsely accused' of some-such harassment?" reported Kate.

"It's a man's world, ladies. BUT I can say, and those of us who remember will all agree, that there was a really sweet man who once worked in the rehabilitation side who didn't do what some girl said he did. She really was just one of them who was looking to get a paycheck, and people like that is why we all have such a bad time." Veteran had become increasingly more involved as the group took on a unified front.

I arranged my thoughts in my mind, so I could present a deep yet logical comment and said, "OK, but what if somebody does do something to you, but you don't say anything about it. Maybe you say nothing because you don't think what they've done does or will affect you negatively, or you can't understand that if you don't speak up, then the person might do more bad things to more people. Somebody who does understand this possibility, even, could just opt out because they can't withstand the mental and emotional toll of fighting against men or courts or laws or just straight-up lies."

"Dang, why aren't you working in social justice, woman?" asked Kate rhetorically.

"Ha, right, I've just got a world of experience being on the downside of it all," I mumble, the gravity of the truth pulling me into sadness.

"Well, anyways, I brought in some Reese's pumpkins for you all," offered Daisy.

Chapter 29: Jessica's Story

The next workday, I found Jessica crying at her desk. It was unlike me to pry into her space, as she had made her private nature known, but my "good morning" had been met with silence, and a stolen peak over the barrier (just to see if she was in) revealed the scene.

"I'm here if you need anything," I offered, then settled into my own depressing, gray area. The office space was the equivalent of a winter's day without snow, in a flat and barren land. Oh yes, and with low-light conditions. I was still waiting on that light bulb.

After some snuffling and a final long nose-blowing with tissue-crumpling and the application of hand sanitizer, Jessica rolled her chair over to my space. Then, with all reddened eyes and creased brow above her mask, she provided more insight into herself than I'd learned in the past five months.

She declared, "I've got a couple of things I need to tell you. First, I really didn't want to like you." At this point, she started crying again, but when I tried to comfort her or tell her it was okay, she just waved me off and started again. "It's just so bad here, and you don't even know. I mean, you've heard some of it, and you're starting to get some of the abuse yourself, but it's really bad. Before you came, I was doing both these jobs all by myself for SIX MONTHS, even though I was physically and mentally unable to do even my own, and…."

She paused while she collected her thoughts, regrouped, and started differently. "My coworker before you, her name was Charlene. Nobody talks about her anymore. It's like she never even worked here. She was here for THIRTY years. And they did her dirty."

Ignorantly, I asked, "So she retired, then?"

Jessica recoiled, then softly mumbled, "No, she's dead."

The entire story was long and horrible. Charlene, witty, beautiful, and intelligent, had all the credentials needed to advance in the Nutrition Department. Yet, despite Charlene's superiority, Miss Sweets had illogically been chosen to move into management, plucked from the lower clerking position. Attempts to complain had resulted not only in frustrating stagnation but also in hostility and inhospitable working conditions. The stress had led Charlene to a breakdown at one point in the early 2000's, followed by a string of medication changes to manage her anxiety.

By the time Jessica had come into the picture, Charlene was a brilliant but defeated woman, enduring years of abuse at the hands of first Sweets, then later, the Sweets-Georgia combination, yet nobody in upper management would listen. Charlene's plan was to work just seven more years, then take the early retirement. She just couldn't afford the insurance on her own. In the end, a heart attack had taken Charlene. She would never see the retirement money for which she had worked so hard.

After Charlene's death, Jessica was expected to return to work with no time missed. They couldn't, or wouldn't, spare her the time off. I was appalled as a coworker, friend, and fellow human being. This poor girl was hurting from losing someone she had known for five or more years and was given no time to grieve. Instead of time off, she was also given the deceased coworker's caseload to carry for more than six months.

"This is unacceptable, and I am shocked. I'm just floored," I confided.

"Yeah," Jessica agreed, "they hated her, and now they hate me, and they're starting to hate you, too."

She told me about the petition she had initiated to have upper management consider my Nutrition Director's application. After hearing nothing back, she and two others had taken more initiative yet and marched to the corporate offices, where they were met with a cold reception and were told, in a nutshell, that upper management is privy to much more information about candidates and the needs of the facility, only want what is best for the facility, and will make decisions accordingly. In addition, they were told, upper managers did not have adequate time to provide a complete synopsis of all criteria to staffers. Thanks, and off you go! Jessica felt deeply betrayed by her workplace. If she wasn't convinced before, she then knew that this was not her forever work home.

Chapter 30: On Guard

The buzz around the office was who would be hired for the six-figure Nutrition Director position. The bizarre workplace hiring policy was able to block my application, but what it couldn't do was block the last bold move of Prudence: incorporating the need to be either a masters-level Registered, Licensed Dietitian, Speech Therapist, or Occupational Therapist. She had quietly changed the job description without Sweets' knowledge, and now she was living her best retired life knowing she made at least one positive change during her tenure. Sweets would be blocked from further advancement.

This development did nothing to improve the already hostile working environment. Instead, there was speculation akin to an underground bookie ring, centralized in the inpatient office. Any qualified dietitians or therapists in the community were thrown into the running as potential contenders. I, personally, had to let go of any resentment toward not being able to apply. Not knowing who came up with such crazy rules, I had nobody to direct my anger towards, anyway. Moving on, believing this was what God thought best for me at this time was what had to happen to avoid bitterness and depression.

In the weekly meetings, Miss Sweets continued to single me out, particularly where it came to masks and COVID-19. In one meeting, I had become emboldened, speaking on the need for masks in the hospital. My mistake was sharing my personal reason for hypervigilance: my mom was a smoker with COPD, and I didn't want to carry this illness to her. After that, Sweets would barge into my workspace, two feet away from me, mask free, barking out non-information, spittle flying out and landing on my bare arms.

By this point, my wardrobe had devolved to scrubs with athletic shoes, so I could strip down and wash everything immediately after work to avoid contaminating my home. If I was willing to give up style, I reasoned, Sweets could wear a federally-mandated mask, right? Apparently not, and her hostility toward me amped up over the issue.

"You must be a Democrat!" she cried as I flinched away from her disgusting saliva spray.

If I needed to ask for an upcoming day off or office supplies, she was operating a week or more behind, even addressing my requests. Finally, maintenance crew members were working in the stairwell one afternoon, and on a whim, I just asked, "How does somebody get a light bulb around here?"

"You just ask us, we go down to the shop, get it, and put it in the light," one man replied.

"How long does this take?" I questioned.

"About four minutes. Let me finish up here, I'll look at your light, and we'll get your bulb right now."

And so it was that I could finally see! With my newly illuminated office and accepting spirit, I decided to throw myself headlong into the work of making CapMed my home. The probationary period was a year, so there was quite a way to go before I could so much as complain about my mistreatment.

That evening, I ran by the Dollar Tree, picking up some printed contact paper, a funky felt board and miscellaneous office décor. Arriving early the next day, I transformed my cubicle into a disco-kittens-meets-outer-space explosion.

Needing to walk by my workspace to access hers, Jessica was stopped in her tracks. "WHAT THE?" she stammered.

"It's my new attitude, personified. Whatever happens, we go with it! Positive vibes only! Kill them with kindness, too," I explained. A Monchichi keychain hung smiling, illuminated by the newly-functional light.

Daisy absolutely loved the over-the-top design treatment I'd applied to my space. She hung up some wall décor she'd picked up at the bin sales. Her favorite weekend pastime was going to such sales. Bin Sales were essentially businesses that bought pallets of random goods and then wheeled the pallets into open rooms where people could sift through for bargains, often paying pennies on the dollar for the items inside. Old supermarkets or gymnasiums were the main buildings converted into bin sale establishments. The boxes were opened at an allotted time, maybe twice a week, and people were let in to rummage through the deeply-discounted treasures. Daisy had gotten brand new high-end appliances for under $20, and she'd gotten cases of hundreds of boxes of candy for $5.00. The deals kept her going back. Some of her friends even bought bin sale items and resold them on eBay for profit.

"If we gotta look out onto the morgue, at least we kin make it bright in here," Daisy said. So over the days that followed, I brought an additional box of discarded paraphernalia from my daughter's early teenage years and added them to the eclectic collection.

Chapter 31: Pooping at Work

"Pooping at work is a great indignity," I said. "It shouldn't have to be, but then you've got people with no sense of privacy like happened today. I was in the single women's toilet. Everybody knows that's for pooping! Anyway, I just got on the pot and was comfortable, and someone started jiggling the door handle! I thought, *'just walk away.'* But no, it's one of them privacy-violating people, and they knocked. There is clearly someone in the bathroom, and they knock! It's a single! I don't say anything except "I'm in here" or "One minute." I can't remember, because what do you say? Luckily, everything came out normally, and I washed my hands and opened the door, and SHE'S STANDING RIGHT THERE WAITING! We see each other's faces. It's terribly embarrassing. I mean, she knows I've been pooping in there. It's just so rude."

Daisy is laughing. Poop makes her laugh. Unlike the clinical dietitians, she doesn't deal with bodily functions all day long, so she was mortified when I first came to CapMed and started talking openly about BMs. "They got cheap toilet paper here, too," Daisy adds.

"Heavens, does that girl have long black hair?" Tanya asked.

"Yes," I confirm. "And tan skin. She's thin, wears maroon scrubs."

"Oh, lordy, she did that to me before. No sense, that one. I told her when I came out. I said, 'Go in there if ya want to, but they's ten other toilets I'd recommend instead right now'."

"Ha! You didn't!" laughed Jessica.

"I most certainly did, girls. Was she born in a barn or somethin'?? Kept a-knockin' at my locked door! I wasn't havin' it," said Tanya.

"I heard Sweets won't use the bathroom here. She leaves and goes home every day to poop," said Veteran.

"Oh, she still comes into work?" deadpanned Jessica. Everyone busted out laughing. You only saw Sweets when she was making things hard for you. For me, that was pretty frequently.

"Wait a second, you guys, what does this girl look like again?" asked Kate.

We repeated the descriptions in greater detail this time. "Did you see her down at the bathroom near the lab and pharmacy?" Kate continued.

"Yes," we all agreed.

"Awwww, you guys, she really *isn't* right. I went to high school with that girl. Let me tell you what happened." And so, she did.

Kate's story about the girl who waited outside bathroom doors began:

"In high school, I was a year ahead of this girl. She had siblings in practically every grade from 6th through 12th. They were *that family,* you know, that everybody knows about. Maybe they run drugs or whatever, or have cock fights for money on the weekends, just rougher than cobbs. Somehow, the oldest brother got hold of a pickup truck, maybe stolen, but who knows? So, they decided to go out stealing and smashing pumpkins, corning cars and busting up mailboxes on Halloween night.

That girl was on the passenger side at one point, with a ball bat, and knocked down an old mailbox, and she told her brother it was hurting her wrist to do it that way, and she had an idea. So, anyway, they went back to their old junky house and got a real long steel post and just lay it all the way across and through both open windows and out her passenger window so, they thought, she wouldn't have to swing the bat anymore...."

"ARE YOU KIDDING ME? I see where this is going. How stupid can you get..." cried Jessica.

"Just let me finish," said Kate. "They were running about 50 in the truck and came up against—they didn't know it at the time—a steel-reinforced mailbox/post and the beam they had across the both of them hit that and flung back, smacking this girl right in the brain. Knocked her out cold, and she ain't been right since. It really messed her up."

"Well, now I feel bad about even bringing it up," I say.

"Me, too," says Tanya.

Daisy, seeing the opportunity to tell a cautionary tale, spun off on the Halloween pranks angle: "These kids was cornin' cars one Halloween back when I was in school. It was drizzlin' rain, and they corned some old man's car in a curve, and he wrecked and almost died."

"So, you're saying we *shouldn't* feel bad about talking about this girl, then... she might've been in on that!" said Veteran.

Chapter 32: Heights

"We stopped by Hawk's Nest, but I'm telling you, girls, I couldn't even get near that ledge! My body was just like, *'throw yerself on over, woman! Just kill yerself!'* and I was scared to death of it. My husband said I was bein' a sissy, but I didn't even care. I said, 'I ain't doin' it!'" Tanya was telling about her recent trip to the mountains and how it revealed a newfound fear of heights.

"That happens to me, too!" exclaimed Daisy. "I'm real scared of heights."

"Me, too," agreed Jessica.

"I didn't know I was until this one time in Baltimore, Maryland, about ten years ago," I started telling them. "I was driving and come up on a large bridge. Now, this wasn't a bridge like here, just a flat bridge over a normal-sized river, no! This was a bridge with about eight lanes of traffic, and it was a big old arc that went way high in the air because navy ships had to go up underneath it. I know you all ain't going to believe me, anyway. But, still, I'm just telling you the truth, that this bridge had no sides, like you could just drive right off into the abyss, and the ocean and bridge were like miles long, and it just kept on going up and up into the sky, and I had a panic attack up there. I was barely moving, going about 15 miles an hour and crawling across there, just trying to look straight ahead and sweatin' and prayin' to Jesus to get me across. It was terrifying." I was breathing heavily and felt my heart pounding as I recounted the tale.

"No rails?" questioned Jessica, skeptical.

"Okay, I said you wouldn't believe me, now," I said, "but it don't end there! I was working at a Catholic hospital at the time, then, as you all know, and later on, I was back in Kentucky, and anyway, this woman from

Baltimore ended up working in Kentucky. She had once studied to be a nun. The strange thing is, I ended up seeing her on a documentary on Netflix about a nun that got murdered a long time ago. She was interviewed because she had been friends with that murdered nun, but anyway (I was picking up Daisy's habit of veering off topic), back to the bridge... when I found out she was from Baltimore, I started telling her about this scary bridge I'd traveled across once there and how it gave me a panic attack, and she said:

'Oh, yeah, that happens all the time. There is a fleet of people employed there whose job it is to drive people across that bridge when they freak out and can't get across'."

"You've got to be kidding!" Jessica exclaimed.

"Not lying," I say. "It's so ridiculous, no rails on a bridge. How could I make it up?"

"I'm not talking about the bridge!!" Jessica yelled, "I'm talking about Netflix! I've seen that documentary!"

Chapter 33: Tricks and Treats

Georgia was named Interim Nutrition Director near the last week of October 2020, and she immediately got the "big head," according to Miss Sweets. And this very interpersonal dynamic opened the door to new alliances. Georgia finally began to see all that Miss Sweets was NOT doing, leaving piles of extra work for her over the next two months until a new director was crowned. Focusing on the tasks Sweets had assigned her previously (primarily digging up dirt on purportedly under-performing employees) now took a back seat to ordering supplies and ensuring compliance with laws.

During this directionless period, the newly hired Jonas was unceremoniously dropped off in the inpatient office to begin his training. In true brooding fashion, Jessica didn't even wheel out of her cubicle. I, too, was slammed with an insane workload, leaving the amenable Daisy to train the boy.

My phone buzzed violently. "NICE HEADS UP ABOUT NEW PEOPLE COMING IN TO TRAIN," texted Jessica, understandably ticked off, as was I.

"Yeah, there are at least two people here today doing almost NOTHING who could train this guy, but they throw more on us as usual. Sweets will never stop this, will she? I DONT HAVE TIME!!!," I ranted.

The entire week ended up this way, but Daisy could not train anyone on the dietitian parts of the computer program; she didn't have access. Feeling generous, I jumped in on the fourth day and took over, regretting my decision after only an hour or two. Jonas could not grasp the concepts, but I was a patient teacher and tried to continue. My issue with Jonas was that despite his mistakes, he thought he never made any. Blaming hearing, eyesight, my instructional methodology, or conflicting information, he, like Miss Sweets, had an excuse for everything, and nothing was ever his fault. When glaring mistakes were evident, he would even deny he had made them, accusing others, including me, of changing his original work. It was maddening. Before I snapped and committed a violent crime, Jessica offered to train on day five.

"I think Jonas told Sweets we were mean," I explained to Jessica the following week when Jonas was sent to another person for continued training.

"Maybe, but he was sent here first to punish us and put more work on us. I'm 100% sure of that," said Jessica. And I agreed. Jonas was just a pawn in a game he didn't even know yet. "When the new Director gets here, I am bringing up this unfair distribution of work," Jessica went on.

"This new guy, though," I started, not wanting to be mean, just honest, "is more like an intern, not a co-worker. Not to brag, but I will—I think I'm a really good teacher, and I've been a preceptor to hundreds of interns over the years, and I've seen who becomes successful and who doesn't. I've got a bad feeling about this guy."

"I am so glad to hear you say that!" said Jessica. "I thought I was just being really hard on him because he was so annoying."

In the next staff meeting, Sweets emphasized: "Everybody needs to work TOGETHER!" She looked over at Jessica and me when she said this, and it took all my power not to look at Jessica, but I could feel the heat of her anger practically scorching the side of my body.

Since Georgia had temporarily been exalted, Sweets finally decided to take an interest in her department, dietetics, therapies, and food service in general. The jury of her peers was not still out; we had delivered a verdict of incompetent with no hope for improvement. But she was also trying to befriend more of the staffers than her traditional two brown-nosing cronies. In my opinion, this was solely a tactical maneuver to add back-up to her side, should Georgia completely turn against her when the new Director arrived.

The screening policy I had written and revised months ago for Miss Sweets was still a hot-button issue between the two of us. However, because she chose open hostility toward me, I decided to bring it up once again:

"Georgia, since you are Interim Nutrition Director, will you be able to push through the nutrition screening policy we wrote months ago? Because Prudence couldn't get it done in time before she left, and we would really appreciate it!"

Georgia, looking proud at the comparison to the stately Prudence, replied, "I will absolutely take a look at it. Please just send it to me after the meeting. Thanks."

Chapter 34: Brad on the Farm

When Mom first saw him back in 2006, I remember she said, "Now that's more like it." She was out there dropping off some Amish bread starter and returning Tupperware lids that somehow ended up at her place. Our Tupperware was always traveling from house to house. He was shirtless in a pair of jeans and work boots, weed-eating on a creek bank. "He's a tall cool drink of water, ain't he?" she mused.

Brad had decided to have a new single-wide pulled out onto one of the small fields on the farm, where he hooked up the water and gas, put up underpinning, and built a porch. He had it looking really nice, and all in return for mowing grass and doing odd jobs as needed around the place when he was home from teaching electrical at the Vo-Tech school and coaching the baseball team at the high school down the road. He had been working as a contractor in Florida and been successful there, but aging relatives brought him back home to work as a coach, and he didn't know how long he was going to be staying.

"Hopefully not very," he laughed when I asked. But the arrangement was great as long as it lasted, I reckoned.

By 2007, my divorce was final, and my ex was sentenced to only three years in federal prison for the crimes he committed. The prison was some cushy, bougie deal with tennis and famous people and no murderers except the kind people are okay with. He had to pay a million dollars, then a bunch of money to lawyers, but what I knew was there was a lot more money exchanged hands than all that.

My son had a hard time with it all for the first few months. He was only a little guy at the time, and he hated me for it, like the whole ordeal was my fault. He idealized his dad and misremembered the way things had changed in the two years before the indictment; his dad had all but abandoned the family for other pursuits. My daughter was too young to remember him being around at all, so her life went seamlessly unchanged.

By the time he was released (early) in 2009, my ex had managed to sire another child with a letter-writing "fan" named Bambi, an aspiring actress and model. Moving closer to his children in Appalachia was now unlikely, as Bambi's work could not be carried out in Steelville, Kentucky. So, there were countless evenings when my renter, Brad, turned into a surrogate father, playing catch with my son or simply just being present. Years in the making, we started seeing each other off and on, casually at first, then seriously.

Within the past three years, there had been trouble in paradise, though, brought on mainly by my own insecurities. The Sight was showing me all the home-wrecking ninnies trying to take my man, while aging and stress (from Loveless, job loss, and Sweets' bullying) were chipping away at my self-esteem. The classic trick employed by the thirsty moms at the baseball field was to use their kids as a vehicle to get to Brad. At least three different women had tried the same tactic. Unattracted and oblivious, he couldn't see it and didn't believe me when I tried to warn him what they were up to, which left me looking like the jealous, insecure person I was. BUT THEN! Within just three to six months, these same women would break up someone else's relationship and their own, as well, if they had one.

"Do you believe me, now?" I would plead. "I can just read people."

I knew he wasn't doing anything wrong, but I just wanted him to SEE what I saw, I guess, and to tell these women to back off, but that might be equivalent to a hot girl saying, "ugh, I've got a boyfriend" every time a man opened a door for her. People knew we were dating, but we lived in separate dwellings and had our own lives. It was a grown-up arrangement that didn't require an engagement. I'd done the marriage thing, and it didn't work out.

Chapter 35: The Saddle

"My grandpa was in the KKK," said Daisy.

"WHAT??" a collective gasp went up in the office.

This whole line of conversation had started with my son. Let me explain. My son loved history, particularly World War II history, and had collected memorabilia for years. I'd told everyone in the office that I was happy he had an intelligent hobby, but that some of his German WWII items made me uncomfortable (he still stored most of the things at my house while he was away at college on the west coast.) If a thief broke into my house, he or she might think I was a Nazi or something!

"First of all," explained Jessica, "no thief is gonna drive a thousand miles to where you live to rob anyone, and second of all, what do you care what a thief thinks?"

"Good points," I agreed.

"I got a German saddle from World War I or II," said Daisy.

"What?" I asked.

"I said, I got a German saddle from World War I or II. It's just in my barn now, see, 'cause I don't use it now since Button got sold—"

"What? Button?" Jessica interrupted.

"Yeah," continued Daisy, "Button was this little horse I had, but she got obese, and then nobody could ride 'er and all. Anyways, so I took Button to auction, and some lady bought her who trains horses like that and all. So, anyways, she lost some weight, and now people's ridin' her agin. Button, I mean, not the lady," Daisy chuckled.

"That was kinda dirty, Daisy!" replied Jessica, shocked.

"But what about the saddle!?" I said, trying to redirect Daisy to the original storyline.

"Oh, yeah, so anyways, this saddle's just in my barn, then. It's got a stamp on it, says 1941 and Berlin and some German name on it. Hold on, and I'll call and ask my son to go out and see." A minute or two passed as she waited on the line, then, ending the conversation and hanging up, she continued. "He says the name is Gustav Reinhardt. Yeah, that saddle's just a-sittin out there in my barn."

"You want to part with it? I know my son would love it for his collection if you do. Where'd you get such a thing?" I was intrigued.

Daisy started in on a long, crazy story about the man with the saddle. He had sold the saddle to her family when she was just a child learning how to care for horses. Soon after the saddle was sold to them, the saddle man was shot to death in a bar fight in rural West Virginia. He wasn't old enough to have been in the war, but his brother was and might have been the one to have brought the saddle here from Germany. Also, the saddle man was a known "wheeler-dealer" and gambler (possibly unpaid gambling debts being the reason for the bar fight and shooting death) and might've picked up the saddle in a card game somewhere down the line.

"That man's name, I don't remember," she said, "but ever-one called him Blackbird." Her side story began. "See, he's called Blackbird on account of they was always crows a-swoopin' down and followin' him. People said when he was young, he threw a stone at one, and you all know crows don't forget. So, all them crows hated that man his whole life."

"So, his whole life, I guess murder was after him, then," I joked, but nobody got it. "A group of crows is called a murder," I explain. *It's not funny if you have to explain it.*

The saddle was a rich mystery. The padding had been eaten away by barn mice, and due to actual use, it was far from museum-quality, but Daisy and my son agreed on a price, and both parties were happy.

Finally, Daisy confided that she hadn't personally known any Nazis, but her grandfather had been in the KKK, and everybody gasped and wanted an explanation, which of course, was bound to be long and drawn out.

"Well, now, he wasn't like that when he got older. He saw the error of his ways and got right with The Lord. But he would still tell us kids scary poems and stuff. Like this one thing I remember him sayin'—he was dramatic, like an actor and all—he would tell this thing I think was from Little Orphan Annie or some such...," She stopped and sat there for a moment.

"Well, what did he say?" we prompted.

"He'd say, real spooky-like, 'the Devil's gonna git ya if'n ya don't watch out.' And he would pause between the don't and the watch and the out and look at all us kids in the eyes, and it was scary like the Devil was gonna git us. But also, he used to say 'The Truth'll Stand When the World's on Fire!' and all, and ever-one said 'Amen,' and 'Praise Jesus' who heard him 'cause some of them knew how he was before. I never knew, but me and this other girl had a school project we did on the KKK, and we found out that he was one of them leaders and all. It was a good project, and we won and got to go to the state capital and all. I got a blue ribbon."

"Nothing I hear in this office surprises me," said Veteran. "I'm just glad I'm an Ohioan."

"Ha! *Southern* Ohioan. Honey, your own state don't even claim you all," quipped Tanya.

"That's true, that's true," agreed Veteran.

We'd ordered Chinese from The Din Den for lunch that day because they had free delivery, and as Jessica and I made our way through the lobby to the exit for the pick-up, there was a morbidly obese woman on a motorized scooter with a shirt that said: "This is What Awesome

Looks Like." I kept my eyes locked on the front entrance. When the sunlight hit us, I was still staring straight out at the treetops.

"Why don't I have any confidence in myself?" asked Jessica. She'd seen it, too.

Chapter 36: History of Sweets

November 2020

Sweets was sweating under pressure. After years of pay for leisure, her ill-won gains were catching up, requiring proof of legitimacy in the form of quality work. Georgia seemed to be turning against her, skeptical that claims made about employees (their comments, their work ethic) were falsely contrived (they were) only to arouse anger. Times were changing. Sweets' go-to response, "because that's the way we've always done it," was losing power in this new climate. She blamed Jolene for bringing workplace failings to light.

Sweets started out in the Environmental Services department, sweeping out offices and emptying trash on the graveyard shift. In the early nineties, employee and patient privacy wasn't such a huge concern. However, breach of confidentiality became well known to hospitals in the mid-to late-1990 when laws were passed to protect patient health information, including how to store it and who could know about it.

Miss Sweets, who was not particularly amenable to hard work and lacked book smarts, saw a golden opportunity for advancement, using only craftiness and manipulation. With not one other soul around, Sweets would neglect the cleaning and sanitizing, opting instead to sift through desk files, personal notes, and garbage remnants. These were the days before the mass shredding of documents. File cabinets chock full of embarrassing details abounded, unlocked. She paid close attention to names and dates, jotting down details of encounters and conversations, and in some cases, procedures or conditions. How much she learned!

It wasn't long until a well-placed comment about an illegal hiring practice found Miss Sweets promoted to a job in Medical Records, earning a healthy raise.

"That woman was the laziest worker on my staff!" decried the manager of Environmental Services, but also, he was glad to be rid of her without filing the mountain of paperwork a dismissal would require. Nevertheless, he was not alone in his skepticism about her qualifications.

Within the first week of the training process, the Medical Records Lead Clerk was irritated. She aired her grievance to her manager, who escalated the complaint to the Director, who, incidentally, was the committer of illegal hiring practices. Thus, the complaint was dead at the door.

The defeated Medical Records Lead Clerk was gone within a year, but Sweets took root, much to the resentment of all who had to tolerate her. She was untrainable, and what little work she completed had to be thoroughly checked and often redone.

After only two years more, the small remaining staff of five, as a group, confronted the director: "Something must be done! We can no longer support this lazy, incompetent person!"

During the years the other staff members seethed and fretted over details of coding and preparing documents, Miss Sweets had been ignoring all the mundane points of her job description in pursuit of more compelling information the position afforded. Miss Sweets saw herself as a Mary and the others as Marthas (from the Bible story, Luke 10:38-42), and she reckoned that Jesus understood her purpose was bigger than doing the work in an office. The other workers knew, in reality, that this interloper somehow was hired into a position for which she was not qualified and from which she needed to be extracted.

Armed with the explosive information she had meticulously collected, Sweets met privately with the Medical Records Director. A call was made to the Nutrition Director, who immediately scurried down the rear fire escape to the basement rooms comprising Medical Records. A deal was struck. A position would be created, with a slight raise in pay and a guarantee of advancement to a huge management salary within just ten years, pending completion of a college degree in nutrition.

"No," declined Sweets. She continued to negotiate until the Nutrition Director PAID for her schooling and gave her fifteen full years to complete it all.

"I'm going to need all the copies of everything you have on me, of course," the Nutrition Director stipulated.

Everything was going along fine for over a decade, with the Nutrition Director's fear and resentment turning into resignation. Miss Sweets attended meetings and made attempts at payroll (often requiring correction) but otherwise set her own hours and enjoyed freedoms no other employees were allowed. These perks she kept to herself, under the well-rehearsed guise of meetings and paperwork, always being out of the office or behind closed doors. Coming and going as she pleased, never an hour of vacation or sick time was spent in all the years she served. Sweets didn't attempt to learn anything about managing people or inventory or working in general.

A mail-order education with a certificate of completion had been attained in 2006, the so-called school shuttering its doors for good immediately after. No dietetic internship would accept Sweets, with her marginal grades and the questionable degree. Already secure in her position, she decided to enjoy the fruits of past sleuthing and rest out her days in the ease of middle management. However, the aging current Nutrition Director was also ailing and contemplating early retirement, leaving Sweets in quite a vulnerable position.

Spurred by urgency and the will to survive, Sweets put her ear to the tracks. She began to attend all the meetings, showing up early and listening intently to all that was not on the agenda. She would lurk silently in the shadows of executive hallway corners, observing interactions. In her unremarkable vehicle, a pastime was made of following certain departmental directors after work.

When enough information was obtained to determine behavioral patterns, Sweets walked into the frontage road motel and, armed with past hospital cleaning experience, secured a job right on the spot. That night, camera and keys in hand, Sweets got precisely what she needed to free her from questions for the rest of her working life.

Chapter 37: Confessions, Confessions

Interactions with Sweets had been brief over the past month, but it appeared she was backing off on everybody except me. On the other hand, Georgia became a fully-engaged manager, blossoming under her newly minted, albeit temporary, title. As a result, I placed my bets on Georgia as a contender for the permanent Nutrition Director job, blocking out her previous alliance with Miss Sweets.

"Can I meet with you privately sometime today?" I asked Georgia early one Tuesday morning in November.

"How about right now? I have about 15 minutes, if that works," she replied.

Off we went to a small interior room between the Inpatient Dietitian's office and the kitchen. I recognized it as the place Georgia was sometimes sent to hide and spy on conversations. I had 'Seen' her there and warned the other girls to cease and desist, making up the excuse that I'd heard a small cough over there. Nobody doubted it because everyone ran on a diet of paranoia and caffeine.

"Can I leave an hour early today? Lloyd Dobbler got his leg caught in a coyote trap, and it had to be amputated," I explained.

"Uh, who is Lloyd Dobbler?" inquired Georgia, concerned.

"He's my cat," I answered, "well, one of my cats. So anyway, I gotta pick him up at the vet, and they wanted me to be there by five, but leaving an hour early here is the only way I can get there on time."

"Okay, but Miss Sweets is your direct manager, so you really need to go through her," she explained. "And also, I

124

think it's weird when people name animals by people names."

Feigning defense, I cried, "I didn't do it. My daughter did!" Sid always named her pets human names, which she thought was hilarious. It all started at age four with a mouse named Gary and progressed from there. No name was safe, be it from pop culture, world history, anything. It was hard to believe she was a teenager, and her brother was in college.

I re-focused my attention on the primary reason for my visit. I proceeded to lather Georgia in well-deserved praise for her temporary takeover, as well as voice my hope of her permanent hiring and thanks for her appraisal of the policies I had submitted for review. She was smarter than we all gave her credit for, I thought, but still had an underlying temper, so I needed to tread lightly.

Revealing my true reason for the undercover meeting, I pulled a stack of papers from my binder (copies, of course, since the girls had warned me constantly to make copies), which I provided and urged Georgia to review at her leisure.

"I have reason to believe Miss Sweets is painting me in a negative light. Here are reports on my productivity over the past three months. You'll see it's higher by at least 10% than any other person in this department. There are two letters that patients and staff wrote praising me and my work that never saw the light of day; lucky for me, they had made copies before submitting them months ago. There's more than that. You'll find all the proof you need right there. I'd like this bullying to stop."

Georgia seemed to care. Her brow furrowed. She asked a few questions. I knew that Sweets initially assigned her to get me fired, so maybe it was some guilt on her part. But, on the other hand, she seemed to be going in a more professional direction now that someone was taking a chance on her.

"Do you want me to handle her now, or do you wanna wait until they decide who's gonna be Director?" offered Georgia.

"How much longer do I have to wait?" I inquired.

She then replied, "We'll know December 1st."

"I can wait that long."

My meeting with Georgia was kept secret from everyone. I was in high spirits, hoping that this nonsense with Sweets would soon be put to rest. Even if she, per Prudence, "couldn't be fired," at least she could just stay in her office and leave everybody alone. After six months of employment, she'd given me nothing but anxiety.

Indeed, the CapMed staff was highly medicated. At least six dietitians and therapists, since joining the team, were on a variety of different medications for anxiety and depression, all traced back to within two years of employment.

"I wish a statistician would come in here and study this place," Erin quipped. She, being never present, escaped the abusive conditions and was, at thirty-eight, on no medications, and therefore her Nutrition Department job at CapMed was considered the most desirable.

"Thank you for your support, Erin. 'We're all mad here.'" quoted Veteran.

"What if you could choose all the aches, pains, and mental anguish from your whole life and pack it into one time period all at once, then have only good for the rest of your days with only death to worry about? Maybe you wouldn't even medicate yourself because you'd know it wasn't going to last forever. If I knew the timeframe, I think I'd choose that," said Erin.

"There's a reason why God doesn't allow it to go down that way, which is the amount I've got now and have coming later is enough to kill a person," commented Jessica.

"Besides, Erin, and no offense," Veteran reminded everyone, "but you work far away from all this drama, so you really can't speak on mental anguish."

During the following discussion over the merits of Xanax -vs.- Ativan, Jonas showed up, and the conversation petered out. He was becoming the new "butt kisser #1," and nobody trusted him with true feelings about management or wanted him to know about personal mental health struggles. So only Erin, Daisy, and I remained in the office, as the others dispersed with work-related excuses.

I wheeled back into my cubicle space as Jonas excitedly introduced himself to Erin: "Oh, I haven't met you yet, but I've been dying to, 'cause I just wanted to explain something to you, so you didn't think anything bad about how I got harred on here!!"

My ears perked up like Cujo's at the sound of my car in the morning.

"We're from out Turkey Holler way, both of us!!" Jonas continued.

"I did not know that," deadpanned Erin.

"Yes!!!" replied Jonas, "and of course, you probably know that Georgia is, too, and anyway, my daddy's a policeman in town, and he pulled Georgia over and was just chattin' with her and all. He found out all about her job, so he just went for it! He said, 'if you har my boy, then we'll just forget all about this ticket.' He's a jokester, my dad."

There was a moment of silence as I held my breath; Jonas likely caught his breath, Daisy was probably breathing and oblivious to it all, and Erin was again glad she worked off-campus.

"Shew, anyways, I didn't want you to think that was why I got this job because it wasn't. That was just how we met Georgia and all. I got the job on *merit*. See, I already know how to do all this stuff and me only here a couple of weeks." At that point, he lowered his voice: "Just don't say anything, but those two cubicle girls didn't want to help train me. They were clearly *jealous* of me."

Before texting Jessica to GET BACK NOW, I temporarily retreated into a Pisces anger-fueled daydream, in which I FLEW out of my workspace, running full-bore, tackling Little Mister Know-It-All as he sat smugly in his cheap rolling chair. I knocked him to the concrete floor and landed squarely upon him, straddling his undeserving, over-plucked-eyebrow-having, Donald-Trump-spray-tan-wearing body, and pummeled him until my wild madness subsided, and I stood, satiated.

In real life, though, I stayed silent, taking in all the details, writing feverishly into a Steno pad I had on hand for all the ridiculous events that occurred there, which someday I may wish to incorporate into a formal complaint. I swallowed the anger down, bitter and black like cheap unsweetened coffee, as I'd done at least once a week since coming to work at CapMed. Is it any wonder I had packed on weight--- not muscle, but cellulite and flab--- due to the thwarted fight, flight, or flee response? All that adrenaline coursed through me, ignored.

Chapter 38: Name Game

Thanksgiving approached, and the Bill Gates pool party game was over. This was partly due to people's religious devotion being rekindled by holiday tradition. Jonas made everyone feel bad by revealing the Gates Family had visited his cousin's Eastern Kentucky elementary school a few years ago and donated loads of free stuff, including computers and books.

"You all shouldn't be talking bad about someone who would fly across the country just to be generous to poor strangers," he reasoned.

Maybe he saw us on American Idol, I thought.

The talk of elementary schools had led to my query: "Do they still teach square dancing in gym class? In elementary school, I mean. I had it, didn't you, Daisy?"

"Yeah, I learnt it. Also learnt how to shoot a shotgun in high school gym class, then they took the whole class out to the lake for a big picnic. They was a pontoon boat and ever-thing."

"ANYWAY," said Veteran, redirecting, "I had to learn square dancing, but I don't think they teach it anymore."

"How sad. It's a dying art," I joked.

"Maybe we done clogging, not square dancing," mused Daisy. "Anyways, we done some kind of dance."

"I most certainly did not do that," said Jessica.

"Nor I," agreed Kate, "although, I did not attend a *county* school like all of you."

"Ha! Bet you didn't do a project on your grandpa's KKK involvement, either, did you?" joked Veteran.

Everyone was laughing except Daisy, who was trying to calm everyone down with, "Now, you guys, I told you...."

"But some things do make me mad, like taking music and art out of some of the schools. I can still remember the words to 'Turkey in the Corn,'" reminisced Veteran.

"I painted a plate once, and my mom still has that old thing," commented Daisy.

Per Kate, they learned "Blackbird" by The Beatles when she was in 4th grade, which started her love of all things rock and roll.

With the pool party game behind us and all the talk of dying traditions, I decided to introduce one tradition that started at Our Lady over a decade ago, the Hillbilly Baby Name List. I found the crumpled paper at home among my memories and presented it before the staff meeting and the arrival of management. Jonas, now officially Butt-Kisser #1, always arrived with management, "carrying their books," so to speak, so I was safe from his interference as well.

"Let it be known to all who can hear my voice," I announced, "as I read the names listed herein, that you are bound to this contract! The next person in this room to have a child will name their child one of the names on this list, or else this group will give that child a terrible and lifelong nutrition-related nickname like Kwashiorkor or Sprue! Now, I will read from the list of names from which you must choose and bind you all to this contract:

Abner, Alva, Alvin, Amos, Anse, Archie, Asa, Billy Ray, Bucky, Buddy, Buford, Carless, Catfish, Cecil Ray, Chester, Chet, Claude, Cletus, Clint, Cooter, Delbert, Denver, Donny Ray, De-Wayne, Earl, Elmer, Elrod, Evert, Floyd, Furman, Gaylen, Golden, Gomer, Harlan, Hassel, Hyman, Irvin, Jasper, Jebediah/Jeb, Jed, Jessico, Jimmy Ray, Junior, Kermit, Leonard, Leroy, Lester, Lyle, Manly, Maynard, Melvin, Merle, Nimrod, Norwood, Odele, Okey, Orville, Otha, Otis, Piney, Ran, Roy, Saford, Tug, Vernon/Vern, Virgil, Wade, Waylon, Wilbur/Willard/Willie.

Ada, Albertha, Clorene, Dicy, Donelda, Earnestine, Gaynel, Goldie, Hassie, Ida, Imma Jean, Iona, Leila, Lucille, Mamie, Minniebelle, Myrtle, Nettie, Oralee, Pansy, Pearl, Ruby, Twyla Fay.

I read the list fast enough to finish before the arrival of the Brown-Nosers and to not allow for too much comic disruption.

Tanya was doubled over laughing and squalled, "My son's name is on that list!!"

Erin and Kate identified cousins and Daisy a grandparent. I, of course, was kin to a Jasper and Mamie, among others.

"Well, I guess that is some pretty good birth control," commented Veteran, "because there's no way I'm naming a kid Cletus."

Chapter 39: Vacation Report

"You woulda thought this Coronavirus stuff would cut down on some of the people, but they was so many, and them laws agin thongs? Well, I don't think they have them now," advised Daisy, recounting her summer trip to Myrtle Beach.

Jessica just rolled her eyes and continued to flip through the cheap paper calendar. She was planning out her 2021 vacation days, and she was going to the ocean regardless of thongs or throngs. At CapMed, you were expected to know on January 1 where you would be every day of the coming year. Sweets couldn't manage any last-minute changes.

Daisy was not dissuaded. "And the tattoos!" she said. "I had never seen so many in all my life. All the young people seem to have them now, and you know they will one day look back and wish they hadn't done all that."

"Now, Daisy," demanded Jessica, "don't you think the odds are pretty good that someone in this department has at least one tattoo, and maybe you're offending them right now?"

"Well, that still don't make it right per Leviticus 19:28. I'm just sayin' maybe somebody got one, and they didn't know it wasn't right, and later they did know, but then it's too late. Regret," Daisy explained.

"All she's saying is people do stuff that makes permanent marks that sometimes turn out okay but, when you get older like us, sometimes remind you that you made a mistake in life. It's not about the tattoos. They're just like a metaphor or whatever. That verse is Old Testament," I added.

"Huh?" said Daisy.

"Okay, you Tammy Faye Bakers," said Jessica," I don't have any *yet*, guys, so don't worry about me. I wouldn't want to tarnish this already perfect canvas, anyway. Joking, just joking."

"Amen, sister," we all agreed.

"And then there's the kind of example you are showing your own kids to be…" continued Daisy.

"STOP," I cautioned, but she pushed on:

"Remember that woman we had in the alcohol rehab? Her parents named her Margarita! She didn't ever stand no chance. So, you do impact your kids and all."

"Daisy, I know you mean well, but can you just let me be young right now? I'm not getting a full sleeve, I don't have the body confidence to wear a thong, and I don't even want kids, but if I did, I 100% would not name them after alcoholic beverages," concluded Jessica. She wheeled back into her cubicle, and the discussion was officially over.

Things had been tense between the two, Daisy and Jessica, before my hiring, I'd learned. Daisy was sweet and primarily passive, but at least twice I'd witnessed her ascension to a doggedly pious soapbox. Jessica was capable of a cold shoulder that wouldn't thaw for months. Breaking the ice between them through befriending each separately, my presence had helped transform the office into a diplomatic environment.

The Holidays brought with them my introduction of the wacky Office Elf. He was a wee little miniature knock-off version of Elf on the Shelf, and Jessica was the first to fall victim to his chaos on the first workday after Thanksgiving. An entire one-foot diameter snowflake built from Q-Tips was in her office chair, with Office Elf, the proud artist, perched alongside.

"Oh. My. Gosh. What in the world??" Jessica yelped. I explained that Office Elf was watching her today, but he would be watching someone new tomorrow, and she could see to that. Daisy and the others came in throughout the day as word spread, and Jessica had gone out seeking a new chair. Everyone was in for even a tiny bit of fun, because you have to make your own in the most hostile workplaces.

One morning, Daisy came in to a Miley Cyrus-worthy wrecking ball performance by Office Elf, hanging over her ancient desktop computer, riding a Christmas bulb strung with tinsel. In turn, I was delighted to find Office Elf attending the birth of Jesus alongside Mary, Joseph, and the three wise men. Unfortunately, the joy brought by Office Elf would be short-lived.

Three of five days each week were good, typically. The other two involved run-ins with Sweets that ranged from unpleasant to scary. She was conniving enough to realize that giving special treatment to everyone EXCEPT the Inpatient Dietitians would ensure that nobody but us two would complain about her anymore, gradually forgetting all the hurts of the past. The Nutrition Director was about to be revealed, and Georgia, now siding with me, would be against her. She needed support.

Sweets began not only telling stories about family members and their surgeries, pets, and children, but she began embellishing about the hardships in her own miserable life. She made sure everyone with half a heart felt so sorry for her they would never want another bad thing, like demotion or firing, to happen. After all, she lived all alone in an old house in need of repair; this job was really all she had going for her. Because she was leaving the others alone, she reasoned they would think it was not possibly true she had taken on a new victim. I started to think that maybe I WAS paranoid, and the old currents of fear rose inside.

Just the week before Thanksgiving, I had been outside my house, bending down, tending to mums when the flitting-in-the-ear jolted me to attention. I felt the weight of a hand on my shoulder and spun around, but there was nobody. Retreating to the house, I prayed for the Lord's protection, grateful my daughter was visiting a friend, but worried about what was happening, afraid to tell anyone. That night, I lie in bed, restless, narratives about Sweets (I can't defend myself against her lies) and narratives against myself (you're crazy, you need medication) flooding in and blocking sleep.

Chapter 40: Code Switching

One of the therapists had stopped by to express her love for the medical resident we'd all nicknamed "Rico Suave." He had come through in the same intern group as "Tiny Feet," a 6' super-buff fitness fanatic with what appeared to be about a size-5 shoe, "Big Hair," a girl still sporting the 1980's bang poof, "Airhead Kim," a brilliant medical student with zero common sense, "Eye Patch," a short girl who'd evidently had an injury or corrective surgery before the residency, and "Quiet Chinese Guy," who was just that. "Quiet Chinese Guy" spoke in a whisper but, we believed, had a deep rage burning inside; he typed in all caps. There was also "Netflix," a girl with a booming voice on par with the jarring and outsized music accompanying most Netflix movies. We had no clue about Rico's country of origin, but he had a very attractive Latin-lover accent and was fluent in Spanish.

"How come that accent is considered sexy, and ours is considered stupid?" asked Kate. "Asking for a friend."

"When I was in my internship, they were like, 'girl, you better lose that accent 'cause ain't nobody gonna har you soundin' like that'," explained Tanya. "That's when I decided I was jist gonna work 'round here, anyhow. I mean, I don't need to be workin' around no snooty, highfalutin folks no ways. They's even a surgeon here who speaks country like me, and he's smart as a whip, and patients love him. It's got nothin' to do with nothin.'"

She was right, but other parts of the country did judge, and I knew that firsthand after working in New York and later living in California. Some people thought it was "cute," but others, usually in private, would comment about the stupidity of the Appalachian speaker. I learned to adapt my accent and speech to match the atmosphere. Brad was also a master of code-switching after coast-to-coast baseball travels with international teammates. Many of my CapMed coworkers didn't travel and saw no reason to hide their native tongue.

"You know what I love? When you're in hospital mode and your family is like, 'huh?'" added Jessica. "Because remember when you first started learning medical terminology and all that, and it's basically a foreign language—Latin, or whatever—and then there are all the meds, both generic and brand names. All the body parts, diseases, treatments, tests, normal lab values, and on and on and on. The bottom line is when I make notes on a patient, not even the FBI could decipher them."

Tanya continued the line of thought: "Honey, it gits on my nerves so bad when my sister tries to be all medical, talkin' 'bout her *'fibromanalga'* and all the *'nutraments'* she takes. SHE tries to tell ME about nutrition, people!"

Jonas burst through the office door before Jessica and Tanya could finish the line of thought.

"Miss Sweets said y'all need to read these here papers about food preparation and handwashing. These is *extremely important,* so sign the book in her office to show you done it," Jonas stated authoritatively. Instead of passing out the ridiculous "education" sheets, he simply dropped the entire stack on one of the dull gray desktops and turned to leave. Back to the room, he continued, "Any questions, refer to the email Miss Sweets sent out today." He stepped out, and the door closed behind him.

Jessica opened her mouth to gripe, but I held up my hand to stop her, shaking my head "no." I could sense his presence nearby.

"I'll just pass these out. We all have to be very cautious when we're making knuckle sandwiches," I said lovingly. I could feel the heat of his anger through the concrete walls.

137

Chapter 41: New Regime

December 2020

"We would like to congratulate Georgia Cochran for being selected as Nutrition Director," the email started out, followed by Georgia's credentials and years of experience. She had almost lost the opportunity due to several past complaints filed against her for minor physical violence. Still, CapMed didn't really care about complaints as long as nobody escalated them past the lower Human Resources level. With Georgia, no complaints made it past this level, despite Sweets' best effort to sabotage her after their fallout. Two could play at the game, and Sweets thought she alone ruled. But Georgia was not the dolt she appeared, just a cunning businesswoman with the long-game in mind.

Georgia had been acting as the sidekick to Sweets for five years, knowing full well the power of connections at CapMed. But, with the title of Nutrition Director, Georgia felt she had risen above that, had played her role to success, and could be a real leader, leaving Sweets in her office to rot. She headed down to HR to pay a visit, closing the door behind her. Donna, the HR Director, looked up, eyes crinkling compliments of a smile hidden by her mask.

"We blocked that stupid twit," Georgia said, followed by "I hate her so much, and I have just been biding my time until she finally gets what's coming to her."

"Thanks to Prudence, too, that old bag," said Donna. They both laughed.

"What about that girl Prudence hired, then? That Jolene?" Donna inquired.

"Yes," said Georgia. "She's perfect for the manager job, and the way I've got it all set up, she can go right in it when Sweets gets ousted, but that ole bitty is up to something. It won't be easy. Jolene could do most of my work, instead of me doing all my work and Sweets' work, too."

"Ah, this reminds me of back at Turkey Holler High when we used to have that literal army of people doing stuff for us. I don't think I washed my car once in four years, but I also never had to drive myself anywhere, either. You just have to know how to talk to people," reminisced Donna.

"So true," agreed Georgia. She had always been a bully.

Knowing why Jonas was hired, I'd lost respect for Georgia but was smart enough to keep that opinion to myself. His hiring crippled workflow, limiting coverage for dietitians on vacation or sick days. Every detail of each note he penned would need to be scoured for mistakes. An already qualified dietitian would have to sign off on the work, effectively vouching for the quality and putting his or her own license on the line.

The pandemic was heating up in the Tri-State during the holiday season, fueled by family gatherings and unbridled shopping sprees. The inpatient COVID population caseload, if handled correctly by management, would have required an additional full-time dietitian but was instead expected to be completed alongside an already challenging list of tasks by the staff at hand: Two people, Jessica and me.

While Jessica and I toiled long, stressful days, the outpatient and ancillary department dietitians and therapists were closed for business. Still, they continued to remain on the payroll, their daily tasks only consisting of Georgia's old job duties (her position was still unfilled), equally distributed, as well as many of Miss Sweets' job duties that Georgia had no time to complete.

The pandemic and resultant shutdowns had created a shortage of many commercial food products, too, so Georgia had her hands full running the kitchen. There was no time for the personal touch, no time for complaints or grumbling. Patients were the priority, not the employees, per Georgia. Miss Sweets would have to take over anything to do with Inpatient Dietitians. Sweets was again in control.

Some medical/hospital/policy-related things need to be explained at this point. They might be boring. They have to be covered, though, so a person can understand why things were so bad for Jessica and me, but why it was stupid that they were that way because it didn't need to be, and why it was all Sweets' fault.

You might recall that I had written a brand-new screening policy soon after I was hired. A nutrition screening policy defines which patients need to be seen based on a set of criteria, how soon, and how often. If well-written, like the policy I had provided, it will also outline how you prioritize patients to ensure you see the most critical in the time you have. A good policy will be supported regardless of staffing variability; if only one dietitian makes it to work because of a snowstorm, for example, only the most critical patients might be assessed that day.

The stubborn and jealous Miss Sweets refused to advance my updated policy, while the policy in place was years behind. It still required full nutritional assessment on all patients with an albumin level of 2.8 or less.

To continue this explanation without a full-blown textbook boredom-fest, just know there was a time when the blood-drawn level of the protein albumin was used to diagnose malnutrition. Medical scientists then realized that albumin alone is not a good indicator of malnutrition. Low albumin can be caused by loads of other things, usually NOT malnutrition. Having the albumin-related assessments as part of our policy was extremely crippling in the age of COVID, taking up valuable time we didn't have.

Each day, at least seven assessments needed completion due to albumin levels, and they were all unnecessary wastes of time. There were also consults from doctors and nurses, and a revolving door of COVID patients, of which at least 6 were on tube feeding, at minimum. COVID was a new illness, and new tube feeding protocols were developing for critical COVID patients. Many were in the prone position (on the stomach, not the back), complicating feeding due to the risk of aspiration.

Aspiration? That's when food or drink goes into your lungs instead of traveling down your esophagus. We've all had a close call... think about a time you were talking with your mouth full or took too large a drink of pop, and suddenly your lungs just violently expelled all the liquid or food in a coughing fit. When you are young and strong, aspiration into the lungs is unlikely, but when you are sick and weak and trying to eat upside down, it could happen, and the result could be pneumonia, which could be fatal.

Policies needed to match up to what workers actually practiced. An organization called JCAHO, The Joint Commission on Accreditation of Healthcare Organizations, makes sure of this by paying periodic visits to hospitals, unannounced, asking questions, and spreading panic. I had written a tube feeding policy within months of being hired, too, but it had disappeared after submission to Miss Sweets. We had NO POLICY AT ALL. So, I was secretly hoping JCAHO would come to CapMed soon. There were all manner of things I'd wanted them to check on.

That being said, we had too much to do, and the other girls (and guys) had very little to do. Sweets, meanwhile, approved telework for all the others and praised them for their dedication and service during this challenging time of taking on new responsibilities. Unfortunately, Jessica was getting physically ill from *our* workload and long hours.

"We have to do something. We deserve overtime, at least, like the nurses," I pleaded as I tried to get Jessica to come with me to Georgia once more.

"Management doesn't care... they won't do anything!" she responded.

I knew Jessica was right. When we spoke up about being overworked and had asked for help in the past, we were given a sympathetic ear followed by complete inaction. Going on strike was out; nurses had numbers, we didn't. Besides, only two of us were complaining.

Before the inpatient onslaught, there were some good times, though, with Office Elf and the obsession Kate and I shared with Advent calendars. The pandemic had ruined most traditions and scrapped get-togethers, so she and I had started in November buying up all the quirky Advent calendars we could: socks, beauty items, wine, whisky, crystals, cheese, chocolate, squishy toys, figurines, beef jerky, jellies, candles, popcorn. Every day was a celebration for us!

One thing I got really excited about around the holidays was Little Debbie Christmas Tree Cakes. Kate was "working from home," like the rest of the lucky staffers, but I was Facetiming with her, having a serious discussion about a real need in the world: "Little Debbie should make an Advent Calendar!"

Chapter 42: I See You

It was almost Christmas, and we had gotten NOTHING, not a present, a cake, not even a slice of pizza or a simple card. This must have been how they could pay more per hour, by ignoring all occasions and never acknowledging achievements or tragedies. Oh, yes, and never paying overtime. I knew the law was being broken. We were supposed to be hourly employees, but "stay until all the work is done *for your patients*" was the line used to guilt us into continued servitude without complaint or compensation.

"Somebody has to work Christmas day, and you were the last one hired, so you have to work," Miss Sweets explained to me, shrugging her shoulders in a way that conveyed a lack of concern for my feelings.

"But I'm not the last. Jonas is the last!" I stated firmly.

"He is just a part-time coverage person and all," she countered, saying nothing more, staring at me smugly, mask in hand.

"OK," I continued, not ready to concede and growing increasingly irritated, "if he is for coverage, then why can't he cover that day? I have been working almost 50 hours every week, and I haven't taken one day off since I started here." I was mad by then and about to get myself fired, and I needed to shut that down and shut up.

"*I understand,*" she dripped with faux sweetness, "but Jonas has a 'family thing' that's been planned for a long time."

I wanted to scream. *This 25-year-old kid had a 'family thing.' I had a daughter at home!* Jonas didn't even work three days a week at that point and still hadn't gotten his dietitian's license.

"Lord," I prayed, "don't let me hate this boy. It's not even his fault!!"

143

When Jessica took sick, Sweets didn't bother to get anyone to help me with the already crushing work of inpatient. I knew I could call off sick any day, but my conscience would get me; Lying was never my thing.

This was the last straw, though. My anger was a laser-focused spotlight, one she'd wish she'd not unleashed. At day's end, it was dark outside as I headed to my vehicle, which was one of the last at the far end of the lot. I got comfortable, closed my eyes, focused all my energy on her face, and saw her as she walked to her car. The flitting began near my left ear, but I didn't flinch. Instead, I stayed in the moment, following and watching as her Honda started up, shifted into reverse, and exited the parking area. The car's interior was gray, an older model but not in disrepair.

Time passed, maybe ten minutes. Next, I saw a motel. It looked like one I'd seen somewhere before. Miss Sweets went inside to a small room, where I realized she was changing clothes: first into white hose, then a black and white dress, black orthopedic shoes.

Did she have a second job? I'd heard she was a tightwad but working as a maid to supplement a salary approaching six figures would make her the queen of all penny pinchers. A dingy hallway with horrendous printed wallpaper was traversed. Sweets stopped at the door: Room 23. She deftly inserted the key, swung open the door, and *OH, MY GLORY.* They were much younger, but I knew them. I knew then what was going on. I was witnessing the past in Miss Sweets' mind, not the present.

Prudence had given me a warning: Miss Sweets would never be fired. The CapMed President and Human Resources Director would have to agree.

Chapter 43: Saved Sweets

Sweets had started a new life five years ago when she got saved, accepting Jesus Christ as her Lord and Savior. She was trying to change her old conniving ways. A chance encounter with a high school classmate led to the reluctant acceptance of an invitation to a church revival way out in the hills of Eastern Kentucky. It was a Friday night, and having no other plans, she'd agreed before thinking. There was no way to cancel because the lady, who had no phone, was picking her up, too.

A West Virginian, Sweets did not travel over to Kentucky often, if at all. In fact, Sweets was a known cheapskate, purchasing a small one-bedroom house only a half-mile from work, often walking to limit mileage or gas purchase. The 1988 Honda Civic she bought used in '92 had 50,000 miles on it at the time, and she'd put on no more than 1,000 more per year. By 2021, it was only up to 79,000 on the odometer.

She had always saved at least half of all the money she earned, which would explain why she never bought new clothes or makeup or had her hair styled despite now earning almost $100,000.00 per year. The slovenly appearance of her hair, skin, and clothing was strictly borne of a stark nature that had never been remedied.

There was almost two million dollars in her personal retirement account. She also had been hired in early enough to benefit from an old-school pension plan that would be equivalent to around three-quarters of her highest earnings. There were no heirs to the fortune, just extended family, some of whom "worked the system," which means, in local speak, were on welfare but probably could work, kind of like Charlie's Grandpa on Willie Wonka, who got up and danced and went to the chocolate factory when the golden ticket was revealed but had lain in bed for years prior while his family starved.

Purchasing only sale items, cutting coupons, or incorporating beans and rice purchased on the CapMed budget, Sweets ate very little. She had watched many of her fellow poverty-stricken counterparts succumb to overconsumption of food as they became adults and gained access to employment, or at least money. She limited herself daily through some poverty that continued internally, living as if there were never enough, inducing an anemic countenance and bent posture. Her teeth were in poor condition. Seeing her in public, a stranger might suspect a severe illness or drug addiction.

Until late in 2020, she would have a once-weekly nutritional shake, compliments of CapMed, in the privacy of the food storage room. She had been enjoying her life-boosting treat in the darkness of the shelves, among the cans and boxes, when she'd felt eyes upon her. Looking side-eyed through the shadows, she could see the figure of Jolene judging her from the doorway, enrobed in fluorescent light.

Chapter 44: New Year, New Plan

January 2021

I knew I needed to make friendly with Miss Sweets to survive, but the only way to do that was to be fake and abandon the things I believed it: justice, truth, best practice in my profession, and so on. CapMed was rotten to the core. Keeping the peace and neutralizing negativity so I could keep the job until I crossed the one-year probationary line was my short-term goal. The complete upheaval of a corrupt system was long-term. With no physical proof of what I knew, I needed to wade into the miry waters of this conspiracy and figure out the best way to end Sweets' reign of terror.

"Not to pry, Jonas, but how's the testing situation coming along?" I asked in early January.

"It's kinda private, actually, but fine, thanks," Jonas replied.

"Yeah, I get that. Just, here, take this card, use it if you want. If not, that's fine, too," I said, as I dropped the business card beside Jonas' daily paperwork (They finally had him covering the inpatient work for a day.) The information I had provided to him was that of a service that practically guaranteed testing success. He needed to pass that exam because if the bottom finally dropped out here, he'd be looking for jobs, and it really wasn't his fault, I reasoned.

CLICK. I'd felt a tiny sharp jab on my back, turning to find the card on the floor behind me.

"No Thanks!" returned Jonas, brazenly, with head cocked and raised eyebrows that implied pursed lips behind the "To God Be the Glory" facemask.

I just turned and walked out. Let him lose his job, then. He could go down in flames with the others.

Jessica came back the next day to find a smattering of crumbs and spilled coffee creamer around her workspace, the hallmark of Jonas' presence.

"Looks like he dropped this, too, and he definitely seems to need all the help he can get," she said, holding up the card Jonas had thrown at me the day before. I didn't even bother telling her the backstory of the business card, because she wouldn't understand why I was trying to be nice to him in the first place.

"Ugh, he is so messy. Mr. Pigpen," I laughed. "But I'm glad Georgia is making Sweets bring other people back here. It just wasn't fair."

"And surprisingly, Miss Sweets isn't being ruthless with us about it," agreed Jessica. It was true.

I'd been laying on the charm with her, too, and it was working a little better than with Jonas. I had made a few inroads asking about Sweets' nephew's wife's hysterectomy one week and then commenting on the story about her cousin's baptism out at Shady Creek in the hypothermic winter. After that, I stopped doing so much work; nobody ever checked it, anyway. Instead, I made time for the unimportant stuff management cared about, leaving the Marthas to suffer through unfinished work, just like a faithful Mary.

Chapter 45: Don't Get Ahead of God

"Well, they's this man. He's a killer, a serial killer, but he's in the jail, and now he's a-helpin' this woman—she's a policewoman—anyways, he's a-helpin' her to find this other killer...." Daisy was telling us about a new show she'd been watching.

"Are you allowed to watch that stuff?" asked Jessica.

"Yeah. It's just got murder in it. Well, except that one time, I didn't like that, see, this doctor come in and, she's a psychiatrist, see--- anyways, she comes in, and well, she went up, and she started kissing this killer and all and, well, that got some kind of way.... Anyways, that was bad, but usually, see, this show, it's usually about this man. He's a killer, a serial killer..." and on and on, Daisy went.

Jessica and I were trying to compile a list of our tasks for the day with the Daisy background soundtrack, which was both hilarious and frustrating at the same time. On stressful days, I sometimes wanted to shake Daisy and scream: "JUST GET TO THE POINT!" But most days, I enjoyed her leisurely manner and wished I were more like her. She survived CapMed with no bumps or bruises, floating along the surface carelessly.

I was personally so burnt out that everything Daisy said was funny, so funny. Like an adolescent girl at a slumber party, I had become giddy due to a lack of quality sleep. Jessica was anxiety-ridden. When Miss Sweets backed off on me, she harassed Jessica instead. I'd had enough, and I decided God's timing was taking too long, so I jumped ahead with my own plan. I was going to let Georgia know what was going on. Maybe she had some connections who could make things right.

I really hated to fib and was afraid I'd mess it up but felt the need to accelerate the process of exposing Sweets. Georgia had instituted open office hours for 15 minutes once a week, and I hit the jackpot one day, with no other complainants lurking about.

"Hey, I just wanted to follow up with you on something we talked about last fall," I stated. "So, this is just hearsay, but I need to put it out there because I don't feel I'm being heard."

She prompted me to continue.

Laying out an elaborate tale with a high school basketball game as the backdrop, I claimed to have been sitting behind a stranger who had horrible things to say about our Hospital President. As Prez walked by, the stranger purportedly commented that Prez cheated on his wife back in the day with a young secretary at his job, whom he then promoted to Human Resources Director, but yet he was all 'holier than thou' on Sundays. This person's friend asked where he'd heard such a thing, and the friend had replied, "Remember that weird Pat Sweets from our class?" I threw in some other pertinent details as well. To make it all believable and as a reasonable explanation for bringing the tale to her in the first place, I asked:

"Do you think this is why my complaints against Miss Sweets never get anywhere?"

Of course, I was implying that Sweets could be blackmailing Donna from Human Resources. I assumed this information would delight Georgia, but the color had drained from her face.

"Oh, my," she whispered. "This is a very serious allegation."

I waited for direction, but it never came.

"Should I just go, then?" I asked.

"Yes, for now," she answered. "…I'll get back to you," she followed up with, as I headed down the hall.

Something was amiss. It had not gone the way I'd planned it.

Georgia was sick. Donna knew all the rules she had broken, and her allegiance was sold to Miss Sweets long ago. There was only one way out of a guaranteed public humiliation and firing. She had to make herself valuable to Sweets once again.

Chapter 46: Ghosts

"What are you doing here? I thought this was your telework day?" asked Jessica on a Tuesday morning in early January 2021.

Something good had come from our constant complaining, I guess. Inpatient Dietitians had been granted ONE telework day *every two weeks*. Meanwhile, all other dietitians and therapists were cut back to once or twice weekly. So the playing field was better, but still uneven.

"Two words: Train derailment," I answered flatly. Telework was rare, and I was missing it due to unreliable internet. "I don't really understand why, since I have satellite internet, you know, coming down from the sky? But I called from my landline phone and was told my internet will be out for an indefinite amount of time due to a train derailment."

"Ain't no way they's a train near you," joked Daisy, and I laughed.

"You know what's worse?" I continued, "I can't even shop online!"

I had a date with destiny, as it were. My desk phone rang the second my butt hit the rolling chair in my cubicle.

"Are you kidding me?" I whined.

It was an outside number, so I picked up, thinking this could be a patient who was discharged but now had more questions. Had it been an in-house number at that time of day, I might have let it go to voicemail, following up later. In-house numbers were typically patients calling down to complain about the food.

Professionally, I stated my name and location and asked how I could help the caller, but the caller, answering a question with a question, sent ice through my veins:

"Is Charlene there?"

Now, it could be possible that this man had been a patient before the time Charlene had passed, but that wasn't my information to provide.

I tactfully answered, "I'm sorry, but Charlene no longer works here."

There was a stillness on the line. Thinking the caller may have lost connection, I started with, "Are you still there?" but just as "Are" left my mouth, the man screamed out from the other line:

"Where is she? Is she okay? Has something happened to her? Oh, Lord, No! This is Charlene's number. Why are *you* answering her phone? This is not your phone! Where is Charlene?? I am going to come up there, and she better be at her desk...."

I was able to calm the caller down by telling him I was a new employee and didn't know everybody yet. I then transferred him to Georgia, who would likely know what in Heaven's name was going on. Scared and nervous, I not only had internal hazing from Sweets, but I now also had external calls from an angry, potentially dangerous man to deal with. The job managed to get worse the longer I stayed.

"I should have told you", apologized Georgia, "but I never dreamed he would do something like this. I can't believe he remembers her phone number."

The caller had been Charlene's husband. I wouldn't even have known about Charlene if it weren't for Jessica, but there was more to the story. After Charlene's untimely death, her husband began drinking heavily every day, trying to cope with the loss. Then, on a Monday afternoon, he'd called a friend and told them he intended to drive up to CapMed and make them pay for what they did to Charlene. This friend begged him not to get behind the wheel of a car, knowing he was drunk, but the line went dead, the plan went forward, and Charlene's widower

153

crashed out on I-64. A traumatic brain injury messed up his mind, and he'd been sent to live in a nursing home.

"They's probably no way he could get to your office now," comforted Georgia.

"Please, at least let security know this happened," I suggested calmly, but inside I was a bundle of nerves.

Chapter 47: Lottery

As the Lottery approached a billion dollars, I explained to Jessica: "This just keeps getting bigger and bigger. Even if 10 of us are in on it, we'd get more money than we could spend. And the tickets just cost $2.00! Is that really gambling?" I was passing that huge lottery billboard every morning, and it became a constant reminder to me that I was stuck in the rat race, on a sad treadmill going nowhere.

Working around the "no gambling pools at work" mandate was easy. We'd just wait until after work, then text only our friends in the department.

"We have to make sure everyone we like is in on this," Jessica agreed.

I went ahead and paid Daisy's portion, knowing she would pull out Proverbs 13:11, making everyone feel bad enough to abandon the whole silly endeavor. But, regardless of her crusade against the lottery, I didn't want her to be left behind should we win. I hoped she wouldn't be guilty of some second-hand sin due to my actions on her behalf.

There ended up being seven people, including Daisy, and those who knew didn't seem to feel bad about it like they would regular gambling or anything, because none of us ever played the lottery regularly. It just seemed like everyone in the country would make a great time out of it when the prizes got so massive. It was like the Superbowl or something special.

"I feel like we should have a watch party," considered Jessica.

In the days leading up to the drawing and then a second drawing (we didn't win the first time, so we went in for a second round as the prize grew), all parties involved

155

convened in the inpatient office daily to share their plans for the winnings.

"Girls, I ain't comin' back. Just know, if you plan to be nice and all and stay here to help out, you'll be all alone with that," declared Tanya.

Jessica agreed, with one caveat: "Oh, I'm coming back, all right. Just to tell 'em to take this job and shove it, as the song says."

"But would you, really," I asked, "because who would even care anymore? The best revenge is if none of us show up—not one—and we are all multimillionaires, and they are stuck here and have to do something for once. So, we rise up and out, and they have to think about it every time they come in here."

"Yeah, don't care," Jessica said. "I'm still telling them off."

"Me, too!" Erin agreed, which surprised everybody.

"What're y'all talkin' about?" asked Jonas, coming in from the hallway, probably directly out of Miss Sweets' office.

"Oh, nothing, just about how large the lottery has become," answered Kate, careful not to disclose any negative feelings toward management to this mole.

"Well, that's gambling. I just come in here to bring ever-one this new policy I been workin' on. Miss Sweets give it to me to do since my job still ain't ready. Just look at it. It's what I come up with that ever-one will be doin' now," he declared. And with that, he dropped the stack of paper on a desk, turned on his heel, and left, not bothering to close the door behind him.

Everyone waited the obligatory few seconds to ensure he was no longer within earshot, when, glancing at MY SCREENING POLICY, butchered and made impossibly cumbersome by this fool, I declared, "I truly hate that kid."

Chapter 48: After Work Pick-Up

February 2021

Tiny came tearing out of the double-wide, dressed in a sombrero and a little white poncho with red hearts stamped all over it. Mom's chihuahua had more outfits than most grown men in the Tri-State. But he was cool, not yappy and mean like chihuahuas you hear about, and one of the few dogs I actually got along with. He had a cataract on one eye and was likely as old as a dog could get. I vaguely remembered her having this dog before I moved to California, but that wouldn't have been possible, right? Maybe this was Tiny 2.0. I didn't ask because I didn't want to bring up sad memories of deceased pets.

"Sorry, I'm a little late. I had to wait on some chainsaw man to cut a big branch that fell in the road over by the school," I explained as I stepped out into the cold air, shutting the door on my running car to preserve the warm conditions inside. Mom was barefoot in her driveway even though it was only in the '20s. She'd always been very hearty.

"What are you all doin' out here, anyway?" I asked.

"Just checkin' my dish. TV's out agin," she explained.

"Well, call the company 'cause I heard tell people been stealin' copper outta older models to resell. Better get it checked out," I advised.

"It's the end times," she again brought up. "Desperate people actin' like this, and this here COVID thing and these terrorists and wars and fars (fires) and floods and troubles. Oh, lord."

I made a mental note not to mention any other things to Mom about the negative aspects of society, lest she become a full-on Doomsday prepper.

"Well, it doesn't matter, anyway, because the Lord will come back before all that," I reminded her.

"I remember when I was little, and Grandma told me that Rudolph the Red-nosed Reindeer wouldn't be in Heaven, and I was so devastated," said Sidney, my daughter, who was standing inside the screen door, letting all the heat escape.

"Mom! Why would you do that?" I gasped.

"Well, it's true, ain't it?" she replied. "That ain't even a real thing. Anyways, I gotta call on this copper deal." With that, she went inside and dialed up the satellite company on her rotary phone. I knew she'd be waiting for at least 30 minutes, so we packed up my daughter and headed out, hugs and kisses all around, my mom stretching the phone cord to the front door to wave goodbye. She always waved until we were entirely out of sight, and I did the same with Sidney. It was a family tradition. You never knew if you were going to see loved ones again. Tomorrow wasn't promised *(Proverbs 27:1—Do not boast about tomorrow, for you do not know what a day may bring forth)*.

Obviously, the big group of friends at work didn't win the lottery. There was a better chance of being struck by lightning.

The final week in February, with 30 minutes left in the final Friday, Sweets sent an e-mail to me with Georgia cc'd, mandating me to manage "National Nutrition Month" activities, including securing freebies for patients and staff. Two or three problems loomed large in my mind: National Nutrition Month was in March each year, which only gave me 48 hours to prepare, and the 48 hours of planning would be unpaid. I was in the top three for productivity, with at least a handful of people in our department *begging* for projects, and one (Jonas) had no real job at all. They had the time, but I didn't. I tactfully bullet-pointed these rebuttals, sending Miss Sweets into a rage.

A new tactic she'd adopted was sobbing uncontrollably in Georgia's office, followed by any other director who may have been oblivious to her criminal endeavors. Oscar-worthy actress that she was, I myself was called to the carpet to account for causing her distress through my falsely-reported meanness and obstinance. I took my lumps in the office of an HR Assistant with Georgia sitting passively by, then spent a weekend of canceled plans sending out e-mails to secure National Nutrition Month donations and shopping for supplies, all on my dime.

Chapter 49: What If?

"Girls, something really strange happened to me, and I'm about to tell you all, and ever-one's gonna think I'm lying or sac-re-lig, but I swear, girls, it's true," started Tanya.

My ears perked up. Maybe I wasn't alone, and God was handing out gifts to others because it really was the end times, and He was trying to show us the signs.

Tanya continued: "I got up to pee in the night, and honey, when my feet hit the floor, it was like the hand of God come down and smacked me silly. I fell back on that bed like nothin'. I told my husband, I said, 'I can't git up,' and he jist said, 'Aw, you're jist drunk from last night.' Not kidding, girls, he said that to me! Anyways, he rolled on over and all. I jist lay there. I held it, the pee, and then finally forgot about it and must've gone back to sleep and all, until lo and behold, I heard a loud yell that woke me from the dead! It was my husband, and he was a-squallin' out, and I now was miraculously healed, and I moved, girls, I mean I ran, and he was in that bathroom and I turnt on the light, and they was a copperhead in there in the corner, and it had done got 'im. The Lord warned me!"

My mind was wandering on down through time, trying to decipher if Tanya's husband would eventually get blessed with the Sight. Maybe it came from snakebites? But, of course, everyone else was concerned, asking about her husband, who was fine after a trip to the hospital since he'd barely got snagged.

Tanya had used the episode as an excuse to do absolutely nothing around the house: "Don't you think we should find the nest and be a-workin' on snake-proofin' this place? I'm sceered!" But her husband said he'd already been bitten, anyway, so what were the odds it would happen twice?

"I don't think you're crazy or nothin'," comforted Daisy. "This one time, I was at the Wal Marts. It was right in front where you git buggies, and anyhow, they was a kind-looking man there. I see his face even now. I knew he was supposed to be my husband, but I didn't even know him, and I'd done been married three years by then...not to him, of course... like I said, I didn't even know him. It don't make no sense, but I know it's true." Typically, somebody would've jokingly pointed out this might just be lust, but Daisy looked so stricken that everybody solemnly refrained.

"Well, I'd love to share," said Kate, "because I've had many a strange experience, but all mine were facilitated by recreational drugs in the 1990s!"

"And look how good you turned out, anyway," commented Veteran. Vet went on to talk about pets she'd owned through the years and how one of them seemed to have the spirit of her grandmother. *How was this possible,* she wondered? She, too, didn't want to be sacrilegious, but some of the other religions in the world had pieces that matched up to her personal life experience.

"Don't let Sweets hear you talkin' like that," warned Kate.

"Oh, I know," agreed Veteran. "That woman is the most closed-minded bigot I've ever met in my life."

I couldn't help myself. I had to say it. "She's the type of 'Christian' who turns people off Christianity."

Chapter 50: Weekend at Home

"Why are you so obsessed with me?" asked the mean girl on the iconic movie of the same name. The question did not pass by my psyche unnoticed. I was aware that Sweets was expending an exorbitant amount of energy on making my life miserable, trying to get me to quit. The brief détente between us had ended.

It was a lazy, rainy Saturday afternoon, and Sidney and I were snuggled up on the couch watching old movies. Yet, even in that relaxing environment, I'd found something to remind me of work. Maybe I was the obsessed one. Tormented was more like it. Before I could realize the damage of a passing thought, the movie was over, and I'd missed it all, worrying about work, talking to myself, hearing voices. I should've gotten out of that toxic place, but I still had unfinished business.

A commercial came on for a show about Amish people who try to live a secular life in a big city.

"Remember that guy we saw last Sunday?" Sid asked. "He should try to get on this show."

"Maybe he doesn't want out for good, though. He could just be in rumspringa. You know, living some of the 'English' ways to see if the grass is greener on our side," I replied. We had been heading toward a craft show out in southeastern Ohio where we passed probably 40 Amish buggies going the other way, presumably toward their church. Trailing about a mile behind was one lone buggy with a single passenger-driver, a young man who was smoking a cigarette and sporting a red bandana in addition to his black clothing.

"Well, why wouldn't he leave the religion?" she asked. "I mean, once you see TV and get to go places and have a life, why would you ever go back?"

"Loyalty, family," I suggested. "When they leave, they leave their family and friends behind."

The winter required slower, more careful navigation and therefore a longer commute. Driving earlier into work, I kept seeing what I thought was a red fox—just the tail, usually, as it leapt away into the night, illuminated by my headlights. It was pitch-black dark. I was no longer encountering Cujo, since it was still his bedtime. I had even seen an amazing meteor shower on my way in that nobody believed until I looked it up online as proof. Other than Daisy, I could tell that some of the girls were beginning to doubt my stories, because unless you're a country person, you'd never believe even half of it possible.

One month alone, there had been a newspaper-full of interesting stories between Daisy and me, including my neighbor's car being run over by an escaped cow, my discovery of a fully intact 1950s brown beer bottle in the creek beside my house, and Daisy's Mamaw's garden visitor (a black bear, video captured on a cellphone to back it up.) I had even seen some kind of UFO! It was an electric-bicycle-flying-machine-looking thing that landed on the immaculate county football field one day while I was on the way home. But, of course, NOBODY believed that one or the story about the Amish cigarette man, and then there was my morning rant about the preacher show.

My morning rant about the preacher show started innocently enough. It started with me trying to get right with God before I went into the office. I had tried to tune in to the local Christian station, but the static was too high, and I searched and found a different channel with a fire-and-brimstone old-timey preacher. He was one of those

163

that used a lot of fierce breathing for emphasis after most words: "And-UH, I say-UH, The Lord-UH...." "Satan-UH, He's real-UH, and he's-a-lookin'-UH, for those-UH, he can devour-UH."

For some reason, I left it on, strangely comforted by the familiarity of the flow of his words, which reminded me of childhood. The message was a warning to sinners and saints alike of Satan's campaign against us all, but for me, it only brought back warm memories of fellowship and simpler times. Unfortunately, it was the program that came after which screwed up my morning.

"This nationally syndicated preacher show came on, and I was closing in on the kayak docks at Branch Creek, so about halfway to work." The kayak docks got me started on a rabbit trail about the time we'd seen a snake there. My cousin panicked, jumped out of the canoe, and sunk halfway up her calf muscle into the muddy bottom. We struggled for 5 minutes to get her out, and when her leg came free, there was a "THURP" sound, and the white Croc she was wearing stayed buried down there. So, after that, we told everybody that Branch Creek had crocs, and they thought crocodiles and were like, "Huh?"

I continued the main storyline. "Anyways, I reckoned I'd hear what was uplifting instead of turning to hard rock and heavy metal on the other two channels I could pick up. The preacher/host said, 'Our guest today is Miss Gussy Farts, a stay-at-home mom and author of...'."

I told everyone the rest of the story. The part that got me worked up was that this was an old recycled Mother's Day episode used to fill in when they had nothing else to play, I guess, but this Miss Gussy Farts said this about women who stay home: "because these moms CHOOSE to focus on their children." She said this as if women who work don't love their children the same, like they put work before family.

Miss Gussy Farts was on my bad list. Everyone at work was mad at Gussy Farts, too, after I told them what she'd said.

"I actually had a book by Gussy Farts, but I ain't gonna ever buy another," said Daisy.

"Must be nice not having to work," said Jessica.

"Guess Gussy Farts and all her friends done married rich men," decided Tanya.

"Or maybe Gussy Farts is telling us all to go on Welfare," said Veteran.

Chapter 51: ER Visit

It was a Monday morning at work and way too busy, as usual. I had compiled my patient list, but I just wasn't feeling right, as I'd told Jessica and Daisy. Soon the room started spinning, and down I went, then off to the ER.

Just two weeks out from my second COVID vaccination, they swabbed my nasal passages "just in case," which is no fun, but my mind was slipping away, and I was above myself, looking around. I wasn't dead or anything, just having some weird, out-of-body experience, as they say. A nurse took my blood pressure, and it was sky-high.

"Probably because of your vertigo," said a petite female doctor. "We're going to give you some meclizine," she said, fading into the distance.

A male nurse with huge, veiny biceps and a receding hairline remained at my bedside. I sang, *"Mama, won't you take me back to MECLIZINE County, down by the Green River...."* Even with the mask and face shield, I could tell he was scowling. "Not right, huh?" I asked.

"Ma'am, I have no idea what you're talking about," he gruffly commented. He wasn't from around here, I could tell. Up north, maybe.

Following medication and release, Brad picked me up outside the front entrance, abandoning my car to the lot overnight.

"What's happening at that place?" he asked, concerned.

I hadn't wanted to put any more negativity on my half of the relationship to top off my jealousy and insecurity, so I didn't burden him with details of my terrible working conditions.

"When I view everything as a whole, I guess maybe I'm the problem," I responded. "I need to work on myself." I couldn't explain the anxiety brought on by knowing too much, or else I'd have to tell him about how I *knew* things, and he'd think I was crazy and stay away from me.

"I don't know, Jolene. I feel like there's something you're not telling me. Ever since you've started working there, you've changed. It's changing you. And the longer you stay there, they work you longer and longer hours. I hardly see you anymore, and when you are home, you're either sick or asleep."

I didn't feel I could tell him everything, of course. I didn't want to lose him, so I chose silence, no response.

"Listen," he said quietly, "I can't keep watching you do this to yourself." He got me settled into my house, and then he was gone.

I'm losing everything, I thought.

That night, medicated, I slept deeply, dreaming of the power I wished I'd been given instead of The Sight.

The Surgery-Free Beauty Dream filled my mind: I stood in front of my bathroom mirror, using my hands to pull up sagging jowls and neck caused by aging. This hand-pulling probably exacerbated the problem by stretching the skin even more, but at least a few times a month, in real life, I'd take part in the ritual to remember the face of my youth. Seeing the difference between what *used to be* and what *now is* seems depressing, but somehow kept me hopeful that if we ever really did win the lottery at work, my looks could have a second chance in the hands of the right plastic surgeon. Only this time, in the dream, when I removed my hands, the smooth, taut surface remained on my jawline and neck. The platysmal bands vanished, replaced with a wrinkle- and line-free surface.

Pressing on excitedly, I moved to the mid-face, careful not to pull my features into a frozen Joker-smile. At that point, my dream self was not sure I could rewind my work, so I stopped after the marionette lines from nose to mouth transformed from deep crevices to minor etchings. I didn't even have marionette lines yet in real life, but this was a dream, and dreams didn't make sense. Besides, I was becoming beautiful, so why would I complain?

Moving to a more hidden body area that needed work but would be more sufferable of an irreversible mistake, I turned to the stretch marks on my outer thighs. My hand ran over a two-inch area of scar tissue, and wild excitement took over as a perfect canvas emerged. I spent much of the dream perfecting my face and body, lifting the sags, sending the bags packing, tightening skin, erasing scars, eliminating stretch marks and spider veins.

I didn't have the power to become someone else, or something else, like in fantasy movie shapeshifting. All I could do was become the best I could be. My confidence went through the roof, and my relationship with Brad was amazing. I quit my job at CapMed to become a model, of course! Yet my life continued to seem unfulfilled until one day, while on a modeling shoot in a third-world country, I spotted a little girl with a facial malformation. I went to hug the child, and when I did, my hand brushed her crying face, immediately correcting the deformity. My superpower worked for her, too! I used the superpower right then to correct the entire condition.

The child told other villagers what happened, and I was run out of the area. They thought I was a witch. I knew then that I could help people, but I'd have to go about it differently, just like I have to go about The Sight a different way. So, I went back home and went to med school with my modeling money. I joined up with an organization that travels to countries in need and performs surgeries on thousands around the world. I allowed myself to age naturally after that because I had found my one true purpose in life. The dream ended.

Two days following the vertigo incident, the staffers came by to check on me at work, and it was established that I'd live.

"I'm weak as a kitten for some reason, but I'm makin' it," I reassured everyone.

"My aunt had vertigo two weeks after her vaccine, too. Might be a thing," suggested Jessica.

"Anyways, when you was gone, we got an e-mail from the President of this hospital thankin' ever-one for all the hard work they done during this COVID thing. And so, you need to vote on a superpower," stated Daisy.

"Huh?" I asked, privately both amused and panicked by last night's dream.

"The e-mail said we're all superheroes for fightin' this thing, the long hours and all, and anyway, just for fun, there's a vote on most-wanted superpower, flying or strength. Those are the only choices they give us," she explained further.

"I picked flying," interjected Tanya.

"Weren't you the one who was afraid of heights and gonna commit suicide off the edge of Hawk's Nest?" demanded Jessica.

"Yeah, girls, but at least I won't die then when I fall off there! And I don't want no super-strength! What in the world would I do with that?" Tanya defended.

"Well, you coulda broke up them two girls was fightin' at the Dairy Queen that time," I said, and everyone rolled laughing.

Chapter 52: Jessica's Memories

"Do you ever look back on your life and think maybe your whole purpose is just to be a bit player in someone else's story? Like, you don't really matter that much? I've been feeling that way lately," Charlene had confided privately to Jessica.

"Don't talk like that! Of course, you matter!" chided Jessica.

"This place," continued Charlene, "they make you feel like you're nothing, all the while making you do everything." Charlene had every reason and no reason at all to feel that way. That was how CapMed destroyed you.

"Listen, you have a master's degree and advanced licenses, and you can do anything!" Jessica encouraged.

"But I just can't do it here, with all my years of experience. They choose people who are complete idiots to run this place! Then we're all stuck looking like a bunch of clowns because THEY are the face of this department. THEY show up in the meetings. I'm embarrassed by them, and I'm angry things are this way!" Charlene was distraught that morning. Years of fighting and formal complaints had gotten her nowhere. "I keep a file of all my complaints at home, you know. I got a diary, too, which is almost 100% about this place and all the things they've done to me. I know it's unhealthy. My medication isn't helping me, either. But I just got a few years to go. I have to make it!"

"What does Carl say about it all?" asked Jessica.

"I told him some of it over the years, but I don't want to get him spun up. He'd come up here and slap both Sweets' eyes into one. So I just keep my files. If he read what was in there, he'd go ballistic. One of these days, I might get a lawyer! Probably that one with the billboard that says 'Size Matters.' I think that one's awful funny." Charlene was smiling now, and Jessica was laughing about the billboard and the day went on as all days do.

"Hey, I said can I borrow a red pen?" I asked Jessica. It was June 2021, and even our minor supply requests were being ignored. I wheeled back and looked into her workspace as she snapped out of what appeared to be a daydream.

She finally replied, "Oh! Sorry, yeah, I mean, no, I'm out, too."

"Everything okay?" I inquired.

"Kind of," she answered. "For some reason, I just thought of a conversation I had with Charlene, right here, and it was almost exactly the same as the one you and I had in here last week. They treated her really bad, like you. She was just trying to hang on until she had enough money. I've been thinking about that and how sad it is. She spent most of her life at a terrible, abusive job so that she'd have enough money to get out of it. The problem is, she never did. Most of her life, then, was just spent being abused, and for what??"

Chapter 53: Jersey Utopia

"Anyways, I was a-tellin' these folks at the campground we met... they was from Rhode Island, I think, or maybe it was New Hampshire; one of them north states...anyways, we was talkin' about where we was from and all, and they was sayin'—oh no, wait, they was from New Jersey, right!"

Daisy was telling one of her stories again. It was the first of March, 2021, and many of the staffers were sitting around, preparing to go out to the areas they served, but waiting for Daisy to wrap up one of her tales had gotten us all way behind.

The morning began with talk of packed lunches and planned dinners when Erin remembered she had failed to grocery shop after church Sunday. This opened the door to multiple discussions: Sunday sins and old-wives tales, "The First of the Month," and preppers-vs-payers. Daisy was in the middle of a First of the Month tale.

Starting out the spiral of thought was Jessica's admonishment of Erin for not shopping sooner—it was the First of the Month now! It was too late!! Per Daisy, some people, right here in the U.S.A., didn't even know about the First of the Month. She continued to tell a tale of camping in a West Virginia state park the summer before COVID struck, where her family had met another from New Jersey.

The family was intrigued by Daisy's skirts, and Daisy's family had never met anyone from New Jersey, and over a fire and s'mores, the two families learned about one another.

"Not all people from New Jersey live in a city. These was from some country-type place, but their kids didn't know about rolling down the hills for fun, so mine taught 'em," stated Daisy, knowledgeably. "And they ain't got the First of the Month there, neither."

"What??" Veteran cried out, incredulous.

"It's true," Daisy claimed. "They was gonna git groceries on June 1st, and I told 'em, I said, 'No, you can't do that, it's the First of the Month,' and they asked what was I talkin' about, and I told them, 'you know, all the people and all.' But they didn't understand! It was like they were from some other planet and all. So anyways, I said to them that all the people on Welfare goes and gits groceries on the First of the Month, and it's really bad and all, like when a snowstorm's comin' and people buys up all the milk and bread."

Daisy went on to tell us that this family seemed like they must've been rich—they had a nice camper, and the mom of the group said she'd never seen any drug addicts around her town—so who knows what kind of magical gated community they came from? They talked about trips to Disney World, and the mom and daughter of the clan said they felt a kinship with some Disney princess or other. So who were these blessed people?

"Yeah, they probably went home and told all their friends about them crazy mountain people," commented Tanya. "But back to you and your groceries, Erin, you weren't really gonna git groceries on a Sunday, were ya? 'Cause you know you ain't supposed to do work on a Sunday, or if you did buy that food, then it would spoil or all your meals would taste bad," she instructed.

"I was gonna say that, but you all always make like I'm the one going on about the Bible. But it *is* true- Exodus 20:8-11," added Daisy.

"Guys!" exclaimed Veteran, "You aren't Jewish, okay. Therefore, anything in the Old Testament might not even apply to you. Like, do you avoid shrimp and pork? Do you walk around with a headcover or wear scrolls with Bible verses in front of your eyes? It's just hilarious that every time I come in here, there's some ridiculous mandate on activity that makes me seem like less of a good person."

"Oh, I ain't judgin'," backtracked Tanya, "I'm just sayin' what my mom always said, but she also said you can't even cut your nails on Sunday, or your house will burn down. My sister still don't cut her nails on Sunday, and one time she was at my house, and I had a nail to break, and I couldn't find my file. You know I had to fix that thing! I grabbed them scissors, and honey, my sister wrestled me to the ground!"

"You see, that super-strength could've helped you once again," I deadpanned. Laughter rose up, fell back.

"I'm serious," Veteran stated, returning to her original thought. "What other Old Wive's Tales are you girls passing down to your children? This needs to stop."

"Well," I chuckle, adding fuel to the fire, "I was going to tell Erin just to go out to eat on Sunday, but that would make someone else work. Also a sin."

Veteran was getting mad now, so I backed off and changed track:

"There was a doctor I worked with in California who was enchanted by all things Appalachian. He begged me to tell him any phrase or saying I could remember from my childhood or even the ones I knew about but never used myself. He wrote them in a little notepad, probably for laughs, but he would just say he wanted so bad to visit here one day. 'It's not what you think,' I'd tell him, and I warned him that we don't always take to outsiders."

I proceeded to tell some of the Appalachian ways and sayings I'd passed along to the man, including "if you don't hold your breath past the cemetery, you'll never get married," "Don't pick the last apple, or the Devil will get you," "Throw a pinch of salt over your shoulder for luck when you cook," "Eat pork and cabbage on New Year's Day for good luck and money," "DO NOTHING on Sunday but go to church," and on and on and on. There were sayings, most of which came from others but not myself. My mom had a job where she had encountered all types of people and passed all the best and funniest along—like "Fine as frog hair," "Lord willin' and if the creek don't rise," "It's a good thing our wants don't hurt us," "Don't tie a knot with your tongue that you can't untie with your teeth," "Don't get above your raising," "Getting too big for your britches," etc.

An hour passed before Jonas made his elaborate entrance, flanked by Miss Sweets. "Oh, well, here's where everyone is… I been lookin' for a dietitian who can see a patient for food preferences," she barked.

Everyone began to scatter, but I couldn't help myself: "Well, we're all headed to our *jobs*, but Jonas looks like a good candidate."

Chapter 54: Let the Backlash Begin

It seemed I'd jumped out of the frying pan and into the fire befriending Georgia. She let Sweets have her say on everything where I was concerned, leaving me feeling completely defeated. Then, the week after I snubbed my nose at her food preferences assignment, recommending the employed yet also jobless Jonas, Sweets amped up her hateful game by sending e-mails demanding immediate action, timed precisely one minute before the end of my shifts.

Jessica and I were still decrying the lack of overtime pay, or pay for time at all, for that matter. I'd been back to Donna in Human Resources twice since January, knowing nothing would happen but needing the documented complaints. Each time I handed over a form, I'd See new information about her nefarious activities.

The final week of March, I sat straight up awake from a dead sleep. It was as if something was telling me, "GET UP! Go to work now!" I heeded the message, hurriedly dressed, and headed out into the dark morning. The countryside was veiled in a low fog from overnight rains, and when I rounded the mountain near my farm, the low lights caught two small eyes. I slowed gradually to avoid impact. A fox, red and happy, with a white-tipped tail, hopped aside to the grassy shoulder. As I passed, she didn't run away, head tilted, sparkling eyes making contact with mine—no death warnings from this fox.

My drive was pure joy. The bright fox of hope had replaced the dark fox of doom. Everything was going to be okay. Death was not imminent. There was a skip in my step as I burst through the office door that morning and found Sweets in my cubicle, rifling through my papers.

"What are you doing here? You aren't scheduled until later, and you work when you're scheduled!" she seethed, knowing she was trapped and trying to turn the tables. I'd taken so much from this evil woman.

"Don't worry, I won't blackmail *you*," I hissed, turned, and walked out.

I walked calmly and slowly, first, then speedily, then jogged, then it turned into a full-on run. I ran in the dark, under the evenly spaced lights, past my car, past the lot, down the trail, through the woods. The wildlife was active, but I wasn't scared. The only thing I had to fear was humans and the things they created. When my mind stopped spinning, and my lungs burned, I returned to the office, clammy and sweating. There were angry lashes across my face from branches and the new beginnings of briars. I prayed for guidance to know if I should continue and, if so, for the strength to finish this battle. I really was starting to see myself as the superhero in all this, the good versus the evil establishment. Maybe I was crazy.

The entire last week of March, I decided it would be best to get into the office early and see if Sweets was still invading my privacy. No wonder she never ordered that lock for my cabinets. Maybe she was the one who'd stolen $20 from my desk months ago! Regardless, I had no secret or incriminating information at work to find.

My prayers after the encounter with Sweets had not gone unanswered. Like Gideon laying out the fleece (Judges 6), I begged for a sign from God, and oh, boy, did I get it!

The morning after, as I made my way from the farm, the first creature—a doe—appeared right at the edge of my driveway, stock-still only four feet from my car. A mile down the road, I reencountered Minniebelle; that was the name I'd decided to give the lovely red fox because I'd spotted her yesterday, and now again, near the ruins of an ancestor of the same name who dwelt there half a century ago. After passing by Minniebelle's seated silhouette, bushy tail wrapped around, kind eyes following my car in a telepathic nod to solidarity, a rabbit darted out and across my path.

Unbelievably, this rich New Jersey-Disney-princess-level animal parade continued on at least every two miles for the first half of the morning journey. There were multiple kittens, cats, dogs, deer, raccoon, opossum, turkeys, skunks, owls, and even a hawk. The usual farm animals, including cows, sheep, goats, and horses weren't even included in the special animal encouragement parade that day. This was a sign from above that I needed to keep pursuing justice!

Chapter 55: Patience with Patients

"You still seein' your fox, Jolene?" asks Tanya.

"Yeah, almost every morning now. I get in here early to avoid that old Cujo and get a jump on my work, and that little fox is my gift," I say.

"Speaking of gifts, I got a 'Patient Award of Thanks'," said Daisy.

"How is it that you get so many of those, and I can't even get one, and I put my heart and soul into my work, even singing to some of my patients and holding their hands?" asked Erin.

"I can tell you!" answered Jessica. "Daisy lets them talk about their horses and their feet."

"WHAT?" Erin questioned.

"Now, you all," laughed Daisy.

"It's true, and I can verify," I said.

"Yes, Daisy, don't deny it," said Jessica. "Just spend a full hour with a man and let him tell you about his corns and calluses and drop foot. Just last week, some patient told her how he gave foot massages. Now, who tells a stranger that kind of information?"

"Jeffrey Epstein?" I joked, which invoked a chorus of "Ew's" and "Disgusting's" from the others.

"Wow, Daisy, you got some double life we don't know about?" prodded Kate.

"Awww, now, no. You all!" replied Daisy, getting embarrassed.

"I've had plenty of patients tell me how awesome I am, but I've not once got an award," stated Tanya. "I don't know if they forget, or if they do it but the awards get lost someways. I wouldn't put it past Sweets to lose my awards. She used to hate me as much as she hates Jolene right now. No offense, Jolene. I know some of my patients don't remember me one visit to the next. You girls remember Mr. Booty Grabber, I'm sure. Well, when I was out there last, I said 'Do you know who I am?' and he said 'No, but I'd like to!' Can you believe that man?"

"But seriously, here's what happened to me," said Veteran. "I just knew I was getting a 'Patient Award of Thanks.' I spent two total hours with an illiterate patient and his girlfriend. I grocery shopped for these people, ON MY TIME. WITH MY MONEY. I didn't do it for any kind of an award. I could just see that they were slow and poor, and I felt bad for them. Well, lo and behold, I spent my own $50.00, brought the groceries back, dropped them off. The next day, this girlfriend calls up, furious, saying I stole her spatula when I was there, that I was a liar, that she was going to call my manager and call the cops, and that I was never allowed to be a part of this man's care again."

"So, did you return the spatula?" I deadpanned. Everyone was laughing except Veteran.

"I should've bought a new spatula, took it out there, and beat the fool out of that old bitty with it," she seethed.

Chapter 56: Charlene's Widower Strikes Again

April 2021

I picked up the call before I even registered the number and found myself in the same situation with Charlene's widower. The hairs on my forearms stood straight up, and some unnamed fear was on the periphery. Why did my intuition flare up brighter with each new contact if this man was impaired, locked up, unable to reach me?

I'd been instructed to say, "Charlene's not here right now," so I did, but this was met with, "Oh, really, then where is she? She should be at that desk. I've been there, and I know her desk. I *will* come up there."

I offered to leave a message, again with the excuse that I was a new employee unaware of everyone in the department, and this seemed to work, but he only started crying and wouldn't leave a message. After the call ended, I told Georgia what had happened and once again asked her to alert security. She instructed me, should he call again, not to answer the phone at all. I didn't feel like this was a solution to the problem and might even kindle more anger, but my opinions, as usual, were quickly dismissed.

Realizing I was approaching the end of my yearly trial period, Sweets wielded the sword of vengeance against me for all the things I had that she did not: happiness at home, people who liked me, looks, style, and intelligence. She knew the one thing she had that I could never take was her job, and it gave her great pleasure knowing that, even though she had secured it in an unfair fight against Charlene and Daisy.

In addition to being assigned last-minute jobs, I also had to endure small talk with Sweets. She would come into the office mid-day as I documented my work, struggling to stay afloat, and would demand full attention for thirty to forty-five minutes as she recounted protracted family dramas. Any lack of eye contact or mention of being too busy with patients to listen to the minutiae of her sad life would end in claims of insubordination, delivered to Georgia or HR with crocodile tears. I had to feign an enthralled interest in the lives of minor family members and acquaintances or be subjected to disciplinary action.

A Sweets Storm always followed any calm at CapMed. She seemed to have an internal battle between good and evil, but evil was prevailing overall. Thinking of her always brought Proverbs 26:11 to mind: *As a dog returns to its vomit, so a fool returns to his folly.*

Around this same time, Georgia began delegating some of her duties to me. Donna had never advertised to fill her old position, which I could not understand, so she was doing the work of two people. If you included Sweets' work, three jobs were rolled into one.

"I have to be honest with you, Georgia. I've told you before that I've got too much to do already," I pleaded. "I've been a manager before, and I know I shouldn't be working this many hours without additional pay. Of course, it's a violation of law, but there is no way I can get this amount of work done in a 40-hour workweek!"

"Please," whispered Georgia, looking defeated, "It's not that I don't care. It's just that this is how it has to be right now. There's no money in the budget for overtime, and we have to take care of patients and get things done. I'm sorry. This is how it is here." And with that, she stood up, showed me to the door, and the meeting was over.

I was increasingly stressed out, dreaming of the work at night, thinking of the work first thing in the morning, getting ready, driving in, and driving home. There was no way to catch up and move up that I could see. It was all abuse with no reward or future.

Chapter 57: Lesser of All Evils

Mr. big-shot Hospital President and I must cross paths. I didn't want to get into cahoots with the man, and even the consideration galled me. Still, I had to understand his ethos because, unfortunately, all the other players in this workplace chess game were too dishonest to trust. I had to keep looking until I found an ally. In the first six months after I'd come to CapMed, I thought it was like a cross between the movie *Office Space* and an episode of *The Office*. While some aspects of those still remained, I saw more similarities with *Survivor* as time went on.

I'd picked up Mom's habit of watching too much TV, abandoning exercise altogether. A trained health and fitness professional, I knew the benefits exercise would have on the stress I was experiencing, but I felt tired and depleted all the time, barely staying alert during the drive home. It was a vicious cycle. I had thoughts about Sweets and her deception throughout the night, about Donna and Georgia and the Hospital President, and worried that nobody could be trusted. I feared Miss Sweets' retaliation. I tried to sleep and failed, my mind relentlessly racing.

Dark circles under my eyes, I prowled the executive hallway daily, hoping for a glimpse of him, convinced that one brief encounter would provide all the information I needed. Unfortunately, two weeks of twice-daily strolls had yielded no results. Then, on Tuesday of the third week, the man I had been stalking finally came around the corner and crashed into me, sending papers flying. He, flustered and apologetic, and I, nervous and uncomfortable, were bending and picking up the debris, trying to put all my pieces back together again.

I could feel the heat of embarrassment rising in my face. I knew things about this man that I shouldn't. As he handed me the papers, I made a point to brush his hand. There was no way we would shake hands as part of a "thanks" or "nice to meet you" in the age of COVID and hand sanitizer. Nothing passed through to me. I Saw absolutely nothing.

"Thanks so much," I said.

"No, I'm so sorry, I wasn't paying attention," he stated. "I hope your day gets better!"

Chapter 58: History of Donna

Not only was the future Hospital President (at the time, only a director) beholden to Miss Sweets, the sordid exposure had provided a service to Donna, as well. He was her ticket to upward mobility, and he was not going to leave her behind in this secretarial Hades. She wasn't about to put all this work into the next guy. He owed her.

Donna didn't really fear that Sweets would tell her husband about the affair. She'd had plenty of affairs over the years when it suited her needs. If her hubby found out and left, so be it. He could be replaced. The only possible repercussion might be from CapMed; she could lose her job if they deemed she'd gotten it wrongfully, and that was a risk she wasn't willing to take.

Over the years, she'd worked hard and gotten the needed degree to match the job qualifications so nobody could challenge her. Sure, if they looked back far enough, they might put two and two together, but nobody had cause to investigate her, and that old fart was still here, serving now as Hospital President, so he had way more to lose than anyone. *"Why does he stick around?"* she wondered, but figured it was probably to get away from that dowdy shrew of a wife he'd had this whole time. Also, working gave him an excuse to be away from home.

Donna had a memory of how easy it was to seduce him. He and his wife had been sleeping in separate beds a long time, he'd told her. She'd heard that one before, though. What woman hadn't? He'd probably had other affairs. Recently, Donna spotted Jolene lurking in the administrative hallway multiple days... maybe she was looking for a golden ticket, too. How laughable. Poor girl didn't know that one was Fool's Gold.

Chapter 59: Memorial Day

May 2021

Finally, a day off! Jessica was working this holiday. Of course, I felt bad for her, but I was so burnt out I had to be selfish to survive. There would be a large Memorial Day parade most years, honoring veterans past and present, but the pandemic had again trumped tradition. We loved that parade growing up, the Shriners being our favorite part. They drove crazy hillbilly cars that would spray water on you, the speakers cranking out bluegrass music. Another group, the "Oriental Band," was fronted by a large, shirtless man in shiny harem pants, like a genie from a bottle. He was bald and tan and wielded a sword and at regular intervals would stop and do a pelvic thrust with the music. It sounds vulgar, but it's entertainment gold. A must-see!

I drove out to McGlone Fork Cemetery, armed with a gravestone flower arrangement purchased from the roadside out of the back of a pickup truck. This was common practice in our area around this holiday and did not diminish the quality or sentiment. There were also pint-sized American flags flying on the graves of deceased heroes and "red poppies of remembrance" being hawked for donations in town by men in fez caps, standing with money-collection buckets at the main intersection. Of course, I always contributed, just as I did with Salvation Army bell-ringers around Christmas. Vibrant thoughts of the old times occupied my mind, and my tires spun, cutting left too sharply, as I almost missed the gravel entry point.

Her plot was on the right side near the fence, easy to find. I noticed a little gold bell and an American flag and wondered who placed them. It had been at least ten years since I'd been out there, I was embarrassed to admit, but trying to stay positive sometimes required cutting ties... isn't that what the drug counselor told us back then?

"I've been thinking about you lately, Junebug," I said aloud. Nobody else was around the secluded graveyard. I had been thinking about the pain she carried and how we couldn't help her once the addiction set in. "I just wish I would have talked to you," I confided, "...I See, too."

Chapter 60: Friends in Low Places

2003-Present

Rowdy was in love with my sister. He'd gone to high school with her and worked as a bartender over in Steeltown following his own exit from the military. So many folks went into the military because there weren't enough good-paying jobs to be had. When my sister returned from Iraq in 2003, her final chosen tour of duty, she and Rowdy got together, but all wasn't well.

I was out in California at that time and was only told that Junebug (real name Bethanne, but nobody ever called her that because she was born in June and was scared of the beetles known as June bugs... go figure) was having some mental troubles. I had tried calling her but admittedly didn't make any maximal effort. I was over my own depression by then but still living in a marriage with a philanderer. Not wanting to be a divorcee, knowing the stigma that entailed for Christians, I threw myself into other pursuits.

"What's going on with her, exactly?" I asked Mom. I was working in Behavioral Health then, so I felt I could provide some insight, guessing Junebug likely needed help at the VA for PTSD or some military-related malady.

"I can't tell ya," sighed Mom, sounding exasperated. "She told me not to say nothin', and I promised. So you'll have to talk to her yerself,"

"Please just tell me she's getting help down at the clinic or something?" I pleaded.

"Well, she said she's doing something or other to help. I don't know," answered Mom, clarifying nothing.

Over the years since her death, there were times I blamed myself, but that wasn't helping anyone. God only knows what she saw over there, much less the burden of the things Seen. Of course, a diagnosis of schizophrenia or delusional disorder would've meant the end of her career, so I'm sure that was a reason she carried on alone. In the end, the years of service, the honorable discharge, and military pride didn't amount to anything. There was nobody alive to benefit from it all.

I'd heard Rowdy had a thriving handyman business now. I found my mom's Yellow Pages book in the open drawer of the table, upon which sat the rotary phone, and looked up the number for Rowdy's Repairs. I walked to a high point on the hill and called the number from my cell phone. The call went to voicemail, so I left a message, not expecting to hear back soon, if at all. It had been over a decade since I'd spoken a word to the man.

Within a minute, the return call came through.

"Jolene? It's Rowdy. What can I help you with?"

"Well, there is one thing," I answered.

Chapter 61: Daily Grind

June 2021

"Jolene's a prophet, didn't you know?" revealed Jessica on the morning of June 17th.

"I'm confused!" Kate stated, coffee in hand.

Jessica continued, "According to her, we are going to get the day off on June 19th! It's gonna be a new holiday, and next year Columbus Day will be out."

"It's not exactly a *prophecy*, you guys, and I'm basing this on the news and history and the fact that we now know that Christopher Columbus was likely terrible to indigenous people, maybe even a criminal, who knows? The truth is, they discovered this country, anyway, not him, and if you want to praise a white guy for it, then how about my ancestor, Leif Erikson?" I explained. "Also, Juneteenth is all over the news now, and it's being recognized in other states. We could be the next to adopt it."

"I'm just saying, if you're right about this, I'm gonna start to wonder if maybe you don't know some things because this wouldn't be the first time you've predicted correctly. Except for the lottery numbers, that is," Jessica laughed.

Inside, I wondered how I was going to use the information I'd gathered while protecting myself in the process. I'd made it through my yearly probationary period at work, but I thought the only reason why was because I caught Sweets going through my stuff that day. When I'd told her I wouldn't blackmail her, she knew I knew something private about her misdeeds but didn't know how I knew or how much I knew. Maybe she didn't want to find out.

Things had been tough since the National Nutrition Month debacle. We had established a routine that minimized outward conflict, but I ran on adrenaline. I thought my body had adapted to the burden of overwork and the constant stress of mental games. Still, each night when I made it home, my mind would already begin calculating the cost of another day at CapMed, and I would sink into the couch, exhausted, some nights never even making it to my room. Next thing I knew, I'd hear the alarm go off, and my mind would buzz with barking commands and droning dialogue and mounds of patient care issues. Over and over, I would calculate the money I was making at CapMed, based on the actual hours worked, and come up with an hourly rate well below average. I had to figure out this puzzle, had to find a way to expose the corruption and unseat all those involved. My strong sense of justice would not let me leave until I'd made CapMed a better place.

Chapter 62: Rowdy's Repairs

"What if I get caught? I could lose my license," explained Rowdy, "and maybe even go to jail, lose everything, and why?"

I was trying to help him understand why I needed those pictures. He still wasn't buying my lame lie about how I knew about those pictures, either, I could tell.

"Is it illegal if you undo something bad somebody else did?" I asked. "I mean, it's really not stealing because those are images she stole of someone else. She shouldn't have them in the first place, and *she* is using them illegally. She needs to be stopped."

"Why can't you just go to her boss? Or the people who hire there? There are systems in place for this stuff…." He stopped talking because he could see that my face had fallen. "You look like Junebug right now," he said, sadly, and then, "she was always telling me things about people, too, you know. Bad things they did. She knew so many sad things about people's lives like maybe she could just see right into them. You that way, too, Jo?"

It didn't take long for cheapskate Sweets to call Rowdy's Repairs. The flyer appeared in her mailbox one day like a sign she'd been waiting for, urging her to finally fix some of those home issues she was always griping about. Rowdy's Repairs advertised the highest quality work for the cheapest prices, guaranteed, or your money back! Sweets knew she wouldn't be satisfied with the work, in the end, and could either get a rate reduction or pay nothing at all, so she made the call right away. The plumbing in the bathroom was a wreck, so she'd start with that.

Sweets had scheduled the repairs for a workday, knowing she could be there. She came and went as she pleased. Also, there was no way she would allow a man in her home unattended. Rowdy arrived, and she took him straight into the bathroom, told him the issues, and asked for the price up front. No nonsense.

"Okay," he said, "just give me a few minutes to check it out, and I'll let you know. First, I need to see if some of this hardware needs to be replaced. Judgin' by the age of this place ya might have some clay pipe, too, and if…"

Sweets cut him off: "Just give me a price for this one thing here."

He didn't like this woman. "Yes, ma'am," conceded Rowdy.

Lingering in the doorway, Sweets looked annoyed by the intrusion, as if Rowdy had caused the problem at hand.

Gratefully and as planned, the one and only phone rang on the kitchen wall, and Sweets was temporarily forced away. Her footsteps faded down the short hallway, and the very moment Rowdy heard her say "Hello," he sprang into action. He was inside the bedroom in two long strides, then down on his stomach, reaching out, retrieving the shoebox. Scared and anxious, he made a snap decision to take the entire box, hopped up, leaped across the hall, and buried the spoils under supplies in his giant black tool bag. His heart was pounding, adrenaline pumping, the same feeling he used to get during military missions. A smile crossed his face, and when Sweets reappeared, he made sure to give her a price she wasn't willing to pay.

Chapter 63: Restaurant Men

"They say women live longer than men, but you know what I've noticed? McDonald's," stated Tanya. It's early in June 2021, and restaurants have opened dining areas once again. "I mean, girls, I never really give it much thought, but how are there so many ritahrd old men down at the McDonald's, in big ol' groups ever' mornin'? They just meet down there."

She's right, I think. I've seen upwards of 10 lounging about an entire section, drinking coffee and reminiscing. Where are the women?

I asked aloud, "Where are all the little old women?"

"Well, honey, they're probably out still workin,' supportin' these fools that done ritahrd early... I mean, you kin ritahr, but the insurance costs too much! Someone's gotta work!" exclaims Tanya.

"Now, some of them guys is military," explained Daisy, "so they can do it."

"I read an article," said Jessica, "about how 1/3 of men in the U.S. don't work. So, the question was, like, how do they live? Well, a few ways are disability, unemployment, and money from lawsuits."

"Heavens, girls, we got it all wrong! We're doin' things the hard way. If I'd have sued all the men that grabbed my body through the years at this job, I'd be a-livin' the high life right now, but, no, I just keep on puttin' up with people," Tanya declared, shaking her head.

"Well, it's wrong to sue people, anyhow," advised Daisy. "The Bible says so."

"Are you sure it says that?" asked Veteran.

"Well, yeah," continued Daisy, "Jesus said to turn the other cheek, and Paul told them Corinthians not to go to court on each other... but I guess if the people ain't Christians, then I don't know," she concluded.

"But how can we really know?" I asked. "After all, there are some people in this place that say they are, but they're evil as Satan."

"That's the best thing I've heard all week!" cried Jessica.

"I ain't sayin' no names, either, because there just so happens to be somebody listening to this conversation right now. I just wanted to say, I think, for the record, it is so unprofessional when a manager hides in a linen closet to eavesdrop on staff. If they have time to do that, how can they complain about our having conversations during breaks which are MANDATED BY LAW??" I was talking very loudly, and the others were just staring at me. I used my right index finger to form the "Shhhh" sign and my left index finger to point toward the space where Sweets and Georgia sometimes hid. Whispering then, I explained, "I heard her cough a couple of minutes ago," which was a lie. I had really Seen her over there, in my mind's eye, leaned in over a shelf full of paper towels, but that would've been impossible to explain.

"No wonder she hates you so much, woman!" whispered Tanya, chuckling. "You don't even let her *think* she's getting' by with nuthin'."

Chapter 64: Preparing My Case

Having possession of the box didn't bring me a sense of relief but rather dread. Days went by without my even opening it, knowing I had to make sure the pictures were there but not wanting to see the images again. Finally, when the day came, I realized that by taking the entire box instead of just the pictures, Rowdy had possibly changed the fate of Sweets and many of the employees at CapMed. I just needed to decide how to use the information.

I woke up throughout the night, and when my alarm went off at 4 a.m. I immediately began thinking again, agonizing, really, about how to use the information and who to trust, and all the work I had piled on me to boot. My mind was racing even more than usual. I was stepping out of the shower when it hit me mid-chest like a punch, knocking me to my knees. The pain was unlike any I'd experienced. This was not anxiety, not heartburn. I could call only one person who could get me to a hospital in time, and only one hospital was close enough to save my life.

I crawled to the phone. Gripping my chest with one hand, I dialed the number and spoke into the receiver: "Brad, please help me, I'm dying of a heart attack… I need to get to MegaDocs."

Chapter 65: Silver Fox Prophecy

July 2021

Week three of FMLA, and I still couldn't drive, plagued by dizziness from my new medication regimen. At least there was less shortness of breath and no more chest pain, but I was still fearful of a second heart attack. My walking distance had increased to the length of my driveway, and I headed to the mailbox, where I found another nice card from my co-workers. I'd received Amazon packages almost daily at one point; I'm sure the UPS man hated me for making him drive all the way out here.

Daisy sent me a fox-themed coloring book, Jessica sent me an amazing spa kit, and one of my favorite nurses sent me a cookie jar filled with treats. The occupational therapists even sent me a voodoo doll to use against you-know-who! I loved my work family so much. It was a shame that such great people had to labor under such a crooked regime. I'd been thinking the same about MegaDocs, too, after the terrific care I'd received there for my heart attack. There were nurses, therapists, technicians, and personnel of all kinds at MegaDocs who were just honest, hard-working people like us, caught in the crossfire of the powerful and greedy.

I was starting to look at MegaDocs from a different perspective. They had rooted out their systemic corruption and were on the mend. CapMed's dishonesty was as yet unexposed. Where I used to speak about MegaDocs as a large employer and single-entity monster, polluting the environment of care with dishonesty and malpractice, now

I saw the caring faces of individuals who remained after the dust of past scandals had settled. Isn't this why I told my son I stayed in Appalachia? If the good clears out, the bad will take over.

Tearing off the perforated ends of a payroll statement from CapMed as I settled into the front porch swing, I wasn't even surprised to see that I only made $10.37 the previous pay period. My paid time off was running out. Also, effective two days before, there was a $9,000 deductible due on my medical insurance, so all those bills were starting to filter in. I could've sued CapMed, of course, for mental hardship, but, as Daisy said, it's *against our religion.*

Initially, I was worried about getting back to work, but then realized I might not ever be able to return to CapMed. The thought of Miss Sweets sent me into an anxiety attack. My heart raced when I envisioned the inpatient office. Mom, who it seemed would probably live a hundred years or more, was worried about my retirement savings, I know, but was holding back her opinions about that until my health improved. She always instilled a strong work ethic in me, like the ants in Proverbs chapter 6. Instead of saying, "don't worry about going back to work," she was saying, "don't worry about going back to work *there.*"

Deep in my heart, though, I knew that retirement was a waste if you didn't live long enough to enjoy it. I knew that nobody knows the future or the day they'll die (Ecclesiastes chapter 9), but I had a strong premonition I'd be lucky to see 80. So, I would try to live by Matthew 6:34 instead, just living for today and appreciating all the things I have as I go. As Mom would say, "Don't borrow trouble!"

Relaxing and watching TV in the afternoon, I came across a documentary on Frank Serpico, a whistleblower in the NYPD in the 1970s. The captivating story overshadowed what I went through at CapMed exponentially, but I felt a kinship with this man. We, the underdogs, toughing it out, injured but rising above it all in the end. But I didn't rise, did I? I'd sunk down, defeated, and Sweets and the corrupt remained at CapMed, and all I had was a box of pictures and files and papers. I didn't understand what God's plan was with all this. I didn't know what I could even contribute anymore.

Chapter 66: The End, Revealed

Everything does happen for a reason. I remembered back to a time after Prudence first left when Kate and Jessica thought my purpose for coming to CapMed was to be Director. Now I know it was, in some strange way, to get Jessica away from the office and make way for corruption to be exposed.

The day Charlene's widower showed up, I later found out he had actually called my desk phone. Up to her usual tricks, Sweets didn't bother to supply any coverage for my job, expecting Jessica to perform the work of two people again, but she, too, was becoming ill from the toxic load and had taken a day off. She had spoken with me the night before, and I'd convinced her she needed a break. Sweets retaliated against this call-off by providing nobody at all to the inpatient office that day, knowing full well that even Daisy was gone for her children's dental appointments. As a result, the office would be desolate. Furthermore, Sweets could take her time examining any documents, hopeful to find written passwords with which she could sabotage either of the two troublesome employees, specifically me.

When the man called from the outside number at 9:00 a.m., Sweets was jolted into an upright position. Who knows why? She had planned an excuse for being in office, *"just helping out since nobody showed up."* She chuckled out loud at that one. Then, on a whim, she answered the phone.

Charlene's widower started his usual line of questioning. Sweets, agitated by the interruption, realized who it was and what they wanted: "Carl? This you agin? Charlene's dead, and you know it. You were at the funeral.

Now stop callin' here, ya hear me?" and with that, she hung up on Charlene's widower, Carl.

CapMed was all over the news that night. I knew Jessica was home, and Daisy had reached out. Erin, Veteran, Kate, and Tanya hadn't bothered coming by the inpatient office since all their friends were out, so they were safe. Names of the wounded hadn't been released, but word traveled fast through the network of staffers who were inside at the time and had seen and heard the events.

Carl had arrived at an empty inpatient office, just like Sweets told him, so he'd gone down the hallway searching for Prudence but found poor Georgia in her place. As soon as her door swung open and she saw his face, Georgia had known she should've taken the threats seriously, but it was too late.

Sweets was next to go. She'd heard the commotion next door and rushed to lock herself in, but Carl was already upon her. Jolene's smiling Facebook picture lit up the computer screen behind Miss Sweets as the end came. Carl didn't dally, stepping out and moving down the hallway toward the executive offices. He spotted movement on his right and increased his pace. Then, before Donna could call the overhead emergency code, he slipped inside the President's office, slamming the door so hard he knocked a picture off the wall, locking the door behind him. The glass in the frame had shattered, a network of broken lines traversing the photo of the Hospital President with his banjo.

What happened next was a matter of conjecture. I'd not been able to See behind that closed door when the scene unfolded before me the night of the news story. I had heard about Carl's hardships but never learned much about the true nature of the Hospital President, aside from his illicit affair years ago. However, I did know for sure that there was at least one surviving contributor to the abuse of employees at CapMed: Donna.

Donna jogged behind a rolling cart down the hallway toward the Nutrition department. She registered the crime scene that was Georgia's office and stepped next door, moving gingerly around the slumped Miss Sweets to a lone standing file cabinet. Unlocked, as she assumed it would be! Sweets was lazy and never bothered to put in repair tickets to have the broken things fixed. Donna tossed armful after armful of information into the waiting cart. Moving drawer by drawer until all employee information was expunged, she quickly exited and returned to her office, wheeling the cart amidst other stacks, unnoticed.

She had long suspected that Sweets was continuing to gather incriminating evidence against her to be used as needed. Well, she wouldn't need it now! Freedom had come, and Donna could do as she pleased. As activity swelled in the opposing hospital wing, she flipped through a single folder. She found her fear to be recognized; Sweets had made copies of all those complaints she'd asked Donna to shred, but Sweets herself had signed the copies she'd stolen, with Donna's signature. Donna would never have been free of this woman, not even after her eventual divorce was final, and that old affair didn't matter anymore, anyway. Sweets had all she'd needed to make it look like Donna just never did her job. Most incriminating of all were the documents over the past six years, including the complaints from Charlene.

Donna was on all the local news channels, a lone witness to the crime spree of a disturbed man. She was heralded as a hero, raising the alarm and bravely venturing out to check on her unfortunate friends.

"What would have caused this man to come here and do such a thing?" the reporters would ask, and Donna would tearily remark about his sadness over the passing of

204

Charlene, which was completely unrelated, of course, and how he became fixated on her workplace as a way to cope with his grief.

Watching from home, I became sick with anger for Carl and Charlene. Everyone else involved had a role to play in this tragedy. I stopped watching stories about the tragedy; I was no longer going to sit back and watch this man be vilified. I reached out to the only person I thought I could trust, someone who knew the corruption at CapMed firsthand and would believe what I was saying. Also, now I had physical proof. Sweets hadn't made just one copy of those complaints.

I met with the ex-CapMed dietitian "Annie" early one Wednesday morning. The news started before daybreak, so we had to work with her schedule, assuring I'd see Minnibelle on the way.

"I can't believe it!" said Brad, "I grew up out here and never saw one fox, but they just come out of the woodwork when you're around."

The story was explosive. It ended up getting picked up nationally, and from what Annie told me, one of those shows like *Dateline* was interested. Donna went from hometown hero to out of a job and most hated woman in the Tri-State in a matter of hours. CapMed was facing a class-action lawsuit, and Donna was facing civil lawsuits as well as being named in a wrongful death lawsuit. Thousands of dollars in backpay were owed to staffers. Jonas slunk away quietly after he lost his job organically, unable to pass his exam in the allotted time.

CHAPTER 67: CONCLUSION

Over dinner with my ex-coworkers but forever friends, Jessica told us all that she finally realized she had been wasting precious time. She was applying to a physician assistant program, and if accepted, would start the following year.

"I am so proud of you, Jessica!" I gushed. "Now we just have to convince Daisy to get out there and pursue her dreams, too."

"Aw, now, you know, this whole mess that happened? It jist made me not even care about all that stuff anymore. I don't need to have no title. My family is all I need," declared Becky, and everyone hugged her and agreed.

The events at CapMed had resulted in a lot of soul-searching for the staff and shined a light on the most important things in life. Some the girls were searching for other employment, unwilling to ride out the media storm waiting at the gate morning after morning, but Erin and Kate had decided to stay on and the take the helm. Besides, if all the good people left, wouldn't the bad just win out in the end? This made me think of my son. I'd spoken with him that week, too. He'd surprised me by telling me he'd decided to return to Appalachia after law school because so many people in the area needed help.

"Are you sure you aren't just coming here to be another ambulance chaser?" I joked.

"No!! I'm doing the good stuff, mom. It's not all about money." Guess he did inherit his mom's idealism, after all.

"I am in awe of you guys. It's going to be a much different place under your leadership," said Veteran.

I shared that I was thinking about writing a book.

"Please, not another diet book!" pleaded Veteran.

"No, just a book about all the underhanded crap and abuse that went down at CapMed," I explained. "I don't know how it will turn out. I've got a story to tell, but I'm definitely not a writer. *Real* writers have it as bad as *real* dietitians do! Everybody thinks it's just something anyone can do if they want, no special training required. I don't know. I just want to do something artistic."

"You know what you should call it? 'The Devil Wears Wal-Mart'," laughed Kate.

"Woo-Eee, that's hilarious, except that I, too, wear Wal Marts," Daisy chuckled. "Is that supposed to be an insult or something, or are you all makin' fun of that ole movie?"

"I'm just impressed you know that movie, Daisy," stated Veteran.

"Honey, I figured as much as you love animals, you'd end up taking a job that had somethin' to do with them," Tanya suggested.

"You know what?" I replied, thoughts filling my mind, "that is a terrific idea."

Epilogue:

Being a low-wage-earning single parent did wonders for my daughter's financial aid status. But, of course, that didn't matter in the end, anyway; a near-perfect ACT score, grades, and extracurricular activities guaranteed her a full-ride scholarship wherever she wanted to go. Strangely enough, her dad's knowledge of the college application process came in extremely handy, also.

After dropping her off in late summer, Brad and I made our way back to Appalachia, driving first through lands as flat as pancakes, then rolling hills, then mountains, then hills again.

He hadn't leave my side since the morning he drove me to MegaDocs. I was released three days afterward. First, he'd slept on my couch, helping my mom and daughter drive me to appointments, shop for groceries. Then, he started paying the bills.

"You don't have to do all this," I told him privately.

"Yes, I do. I love you," he'd responded, tears in his eyes.

I would be making my first wildlife documentary that Fall.

"They's no money in that, is there, Jolene?" and "You don't want to rely on a man to take care of you, do you?" were Mom's two big questions.

I reassured her. "I saved a lot of money when I worked at Our Lady. We didn't live the high life or nuthin'. Besides, *your granddaughter* got a full-ride to college, so no worries there. Plus, she gets to edit all the film as a project for one of her classes, so it's a win-win situation." Stephen Covey's wisdom was still in my life, just on a less managerial level.

In the evening, while Brad was out on the tractor cutting the big field where his trailer once stood, I made my way to the outbuilding, unlocking the ancient padlock, the door creaking on its hinges. I was armed with a spray can of Raid. Allergic to bees, Brad steered clear of my "she shed," a haven for wasps and the stray hornet.

After the frenzy of killing ended, I stepped fully inside the enclosure, propping the door open with an old broom handle to let in some light. Plastic totes of holiday paper, craft supplies, ornaments, and lights were scooted aside as I made my way to the back right corner. The boxes marked with my sons' and daughters' names, brought over 17 years ago in that rickety U-Haul, sat, stacked in five neat columns. Unopened for as many years, duct tape was permanently melded to the cardboard squares. The Exacto knife blade extended as I carefully sliced through a seam and peered inside at my retirement plan.

Made in the USA
Columbia, SC
10 February 2022